A Story of River

Tales from Nōl'Deron

Lana Axe

AxeLord Publications
ISBN-10: 0615821537
ISBN-13: 978-0615821535
Cover Art by Michael Gauss

For Dad, my hero.

Prologue

"I'm sorry, Yillmara," the young elf maid said as she wept. "The child does not live." She held the tiny bundle toward his mother, who slowly took him from the maid's arms. Yillmara looked upon the lifeless face of her tiny son and wept softly. She closed her eyes and pressed him to her breast. After a moment, though still exhausted from the birth, she rose from her bed with her son in her arms.

"You mustn't, my lady! You need to rest!" The maid pleaded with her and touched her arm as if to stop her, but Yillmara continued walking. She made her way from her rooms and stepped out into the light of the dawn. It was a cool spring morning, and the sound of the river danced throughout the forest that was home to Yillmara's people, the Westerling Elves.

Yillmara approached the river slowly, earnestly. She trod lightly so not to offend the Spirit of the river. With her son still in her arms, she walked into the water and fell to her knees, begging for the life of her child. "River Spirit, hear my plea and grant my son his life. He deserves the chance to live, to grow, and to know the beauty of this forest. He should be given the chance to hear the music of the river."

Slowly, she placed the lifeless body of her son into the water. Hoping for an answer from the River Spirit was foolish, she knew, but what matter was that compared to the life of her child. She covered her eyes and wept. As her tears hit the water, she heard a soft voice around her. It caressed her and consoled her grief. The River Spirit had come. The young mother's weeping ceased, and she felt pure serenity. "I will gladly trade my life for his," she said with all the strength of her heart.

With that assurance, the Spirit granted her request. The mother slid gently down into the river, and the child opened his sapphire eyes. The young maid came running to the river's edge along with Yillmara's life mate. The maid took the child from the river and rushed him inside to get him warm.

Though he knew his love's body would fade into the river, Ryllak waded into the water to be near her.

He could see her lying serenely in the water, her face peaceful as if sleeping. Reaching his arms out for her came naturally, but it was no use. He could no longer touch his beautiful Yillmara. She was gone forever.

The river had granted the child his life, and in time, the river would reclaim him.

Chapter 1

"Far you must travel to a land of spring and bring back the River who dwells there." The bent old man's voice was raspy and strained but his resolve was strong. He had held the gift of prophecy for many long years and had served the kings of Na'zora his entire life. He had always been cryptic, but he was never wrong. If King Aelryk was to survive this new threat and save his people from a life of servitude, he would have to figure out how to bring a river from a distant land.

King Aelryk's face was contemplative. He may as well have been asked to move a mountain. For months now, dark creatures had been leaving the Wildlands and attacking Na'zora. Villages near the border were being raided, and citizens were being taken. Aelryk feared a dark force had arisen and bound these creatures to an evil purpose. His armies would arrive either too late or in time to be slaughtered themselves. This was no simple foe he was facing. His own mages had confirmed there were incredibly strong enchantments at work here.

Aelryk stood, immediately followed by his mages. He was taller than all of them, dark-haired, and muscular. He was an expert swordsman and a brave war leader. During his father's reign, he had secured peace with some of the clans who inhabit the Wildlands. The Wild Elves fought savagely, but in the end Aelryk's forces were victorious. The vicious attacks stopped, and the Wild Elves were driven off to their forests. Orzi the prophet had come through in his father's time of need, and if Aelryk could manage to complete this seemingly impossible task, he may be able to save his people.

"Does anyone know of a land of spring?" Aelryk asked. His dark eyes looked at his mages, who each lowered their head in turn. No one knew. "Repeat this prophecy to my historians. Tell them not to stop searching until they've figured out where it is I must go." A young page dashed from the room to carry out the king's command. "Orzi, is it imperative that I go myself? It seems so dangerous to leave my people in this time of need. I would much rather move closer to the border and deal with these creatures myself."

Orzi had sunk into his chair, exhausted from the mental strain his gift of prophecy caused him. Slowly, he began to speak. "Yes, your majesty. Only you will be able to bring back this river. If you do not go yourself, your kingdom will fall to darkness."

The matter was settled. Aelryk would leave his kingdom in the hands of his most trusted advisors and generals. With his whole heart he was determined to protect his people, even if it meant leaving them.

As he walked the stone floor of his palace his mind wandered to the memory of the mutilated bodies that had been brought back for him to see. Many of them were torn into several pieces. These creatures had attacked with such savagery that it was impossible to believe it could have been any beast known to man. These were dark creatures controlled by some evil force. The few who managed to survive were incredibly lucky. In their accounts, they had run but had not been pursued. They had witnessed many citizens being cut down with vicious claws while others were dragged away completely unharmed. For what purpose could these monsters take the living?

Why were they murdering with such ferocity? Where had they come from and who were they serving?

The witnesses had described them as standing a head and shoulders taller than any man, dark blue-black skin, patches of wiry dark fur, huge fangs, and long scythe-like claws. Their eyes were golden and glowing, and their snouts were short and flat with wide nostrils. Small pointed ears sat atop their heads. In all his years, Aelryk had never heard of such creatures. His historians were at a loss to find any record of such a creature ever being described.

As he reached his council chambers, he could already hear the mixed voices of his twelve advisors coming from within. He stepped inside, and immediately his men quieted. They moved to stand behind their chairs and bowed their heads until Aelryk was seated at the head of the table and motioned for them to sit as well. "The Prophet Orzi has given me hope. He knows how I am to defeat these vicious creatures who have been attacking my people. Unfortunately, I know not exactly what is to be done, but with help from my historians I'm sure this mystery will be solved soon. Is there any news from the outlying villages?"

"No attacks have been reported for three days now." General Morek's voice sounded relieved. "The remains of one creature have arrived and are awaiting inspection by the mages."

Aelryk turned to his mages. "I will leave you to your work, then. You are dismissed." The three mages stood, bowed, and left the room without a word. A grave task lay before them.

Chapter 2

"I won't do it. They're murderers. They're not to be trusted!" Mel didn't care that he was raising his voice at the clan overseer. He detested the men of Na'zora, and he would never forgive their crimes against his people.

"Yes you will. You will go without a doubt," the overseer said with a smug sense of satisfaction. "Thinal is going."

Mel glanced over at Thinal. Her dark eyes turned to Mel and danced with playfulness as her mouth turned up into a mischievous grin. Mel was speechless with frustration. He stormed from the overseer's hut.

"Mel, wait!" Thinal had followed him from the hut. "You're not really mad are you?"

Mel sighed and looked up at his mate. "You know I could never really be mad at you, but this is

15

dangerous. These men can't be trusted. The best we can hope for is an easy chance to kill them all."

"Oh, Mel. Where's your sense of adventure?" She took his hands in hers and laughed playfully. "There has been peace for many years now. They have tried to make amends, and they've been fair with us. I'm not defending the past, but I don't see any reason to fear them now."

"I'm not afraid!" he shouted. Lowering his voice, he added, "I just don't trust them. We're expendable to them. We can't expect their help if trouble finds us in the Wildlands."

"You mean *when* it finds us." She smiled and drew her sword from her back. "Don't worry, love. I'll protect you."

Mel laughed and threw an arm around her waist, drawing her towards him. He kissed her passionately, and all his reservations about the upcoming journey fell away. His love for Thinal was much stronger than any emotion he had felt. She was impulsive and adventurous, his exact opposite, but he loved her. If she was going, he would always follow.

"So," she said. "Should we get back in there and start planning for our trip?"

"They can wait an hour or two." He grinned and led her towards their hut. Making love with Thinal was far more important than planning a trip with a couple of human emissaries.

The men had come seeking aid from the Wild Elves. They needed scouts who could track and locate the monsters now inhabiting the Wildlands. There was no better scout than Mel.

* * * * *

Afternoon came as Mel and Thinal lay in each other's arms. Thinal awoke and kissed Mel on the nose. He stirred and rolled onto his back. "Wake up, sleepy!" She slapped him on the chest. He startled awake and sat straight up. Thinal got out of the bed and began to dress. "Come on now," she said. "We have a journey to prepare for."

Mel slowly left the bed and began to dress. "Maybe they'll decide they don't trust us and they'll piss off back home." He knew they wouldn't. All Wild Elves were experts on the forests and the creatures that dwell within it. New creatures, evil ones, had begun appearing. So far they had left the Wild Elves in peace, but traders at the borderlands had sent word of the beasts attacking the outlying villages of Na'zora. With his own eyes, Mel had seen these beasts passing north of the Elven border. They were surely driven by some unnatural force. Not once did he see them stop to take food or drink. They ran on towards Na'zora, and if the rumors could be believed, slaughtered the humans relentlessly and dragged others away.

Together they walked out of their hut and saw preparations being made for the evening feast. The emissaries from Na'zora were being treated as honored guests. Mel was disgusted. Here were representatives from a kingdom that had slaughtered his kind in the past. Now they pretended to be friends. They brought fine gifts with them including some jewels and fancy metal dishes. He wondered what good such things could possibly do for his people. Such gifts were entirely useless to them. Everything the Silver Birch Clan needed was supplied by its members. Food, shelter, clothing, weapons, and tools were all they needed. Spice and sugar gifts would have been acceptable. But these items he could get trading furs at the borderland markets. He didn't need emissaries to bring them.

The Overseer was sitting on a woven chair outside his hut. He beckoned with his hand for Mel and Thinal to come over. Mel contemplated stabbing himself in the thigh to avoid the upcoming conversation. *Just suck it up*, he thought. Thinal was excited about the chance for adventure, and as usual, Mel would indulge her. He could never refuse his love anything.

"Mel, I'd like you to meet the emissaries from Na'zora." He gestured to the two men seated on a low log bench to his right. "This is Loren and that is Mi'tal. You will be helping them track the unfamiliar beasts in hopes of finding their kidnapped citizens."

"Surely there are others coming as well," Mi'tal said.

"No, just Mel and his mate Thinal. Mel is an excellent tracker and Thinal is our finest sword maiden. You may consider her help a bonus." The Overseer smiled smugly at the men.

Mi'tal looked back at Loren, and they both seemed disappointed. One scout, even a very clever one, to cover all the Wildlands wasn't going to be a speedy process.

"Don't look so disappointed," Mel said. "I already know where your citizens have been taken. I've seen the creatures heading in and out of Al'marr."

Loren rose to his feet, his temper flaring. "You've seen this and made no attempt to stop it?" he shouted. "Coward!" The two guards who had been standing around observing the other elves' activities took notice of Loren's tone and came to his side.

Their hands rested on their swords in preparation for a fight.

Mel drew his knives from his belt as the Overseer stood and said, "Please, let's be reasonable here. My Lord Loren, you can't expect one elf to fight an entire pack of ferocious beasts. A few of our clansmen have seen these creatures, but all of them were alone at the time. We hunt using stealth, but once an arrow is loosed, all hope for secrecy is gone. Then one must face whatever threat is in front of him. You cannot expect a solitary hunter to carry out a rescue attempt."

"Forgive me." Loren looked down at the ground and then back to Mel. "I understand, and I apologize for my behavior." The guards became visibly more relaxed as their hands moved away from their swords and hung casually at their sides.

Slowly, Mel sheathed his knives. "The bigger question is, what do you expect me to do?"

Mi'tal spoke this time. "We need to get a basic idea of these creatures. We need to know their movements, their behavior, and where exactly they are hiding our citizens. Most importantly, we must learn if the kidnapped citizens are being kept alive somewhere that we might rescue them."

"Seriously? You've come all this way for that? I find it difficult to believe you have no scouts among men who are capable." Mel was more than a little annoyed.

"There are no men in Na'zora with such an in-depth knowledge of the Wildlands. We patrol near our borders, but we very rarely venture far beyond that. Your people are knowledgeable of the area and highly skilled in tracking, so we've come to you. I can promise you that King Aelryk will reward you greatly for your help."

The Overseer, who had been sitting quietly, finally spoke up. "We ask for no other reward than the continuation of peace with your kingdom."

"No," Mel said. "If I'm the one going, I ask for the reward of settlements for my people anywhere within the Wildlands. You have restricted us here in these forests and declared the rest of the Wildlands as off limits except for hunting. Our numbers are growing since the wars have stopped, and we need more land to settle. If I provide this service and help you to save the lives of your people, I will expect your king to consider my request."

"You have my oath, Mel," Mi'tal said. "You will have an audience with my king as soon as this matter is settled." His blue eyes seemed sincere, and he extended his hand towards Mel. Mel nodded and shook Mi'tal's hand. He did not trust men, but he was willing to give this one a chance. There was no way to talk Thinal out of going on this journey, so he may as well try to make the best of it.

Chapter 3

As she did every morning, Lenora stood at the riverbank and watched her life mate perform his morning ritual. He stood naked in waist-deep water at the base of a small waterfall. Despite watching this ritual for over eight hundred years, she still could not help but worry. His life was a gift from the river, and each day he offered it back. She knew that one day the river would claim him.

His long brown hair flowed carelessly at the water's surface. Though his back was facing her, Lenora could see that River had completed his offering and was conversing with the water's Spirit. Many times the Spirit had granted him visions to aid their people. They knew when danger was drawing near and also when the rains would come. The Westerling Vale was a beautiful and magical place, thanks to the Spirit's presence.

River turned and smiled at Lenora. Coming up from the water, he touched her chin and kissed her softly on her lips. She welcomed the kiss and enjoyed the warmth of his lips. After helping him on with his robe and placing a silver ring with a sapphire stone on his left hand, she put her arm in his and said, "Did the Spirit give you good news?"

"Today's news is somewhat troubling," he began. "I am not exactly sure what to make of it. It would be best if I called a meeting of the Elders and discussed it with them. Perhaps one of them can identify the creatures I saw." He paused for a second and then asked, "Have you ever heard of a dark man-like creature with long curving claws? They seem very unfriendly but have so far avoided entering or crossing the river."

Lenora thought about it as they continued walking towards the village. "I don't believe I ever studied such a thing. I hope they aren't a threat to us."

River stopped and looked into her pale eyes but said nothing. "You seem troubled," she said, breaking the silence. "What is it?"

"It's just a feeling. Something is wrong, but I don't know what it is yet." He took both of her hands and kissed her cheek. "Do not worry, my love. The

Elders will know what to do. I'll speak with them immediately."

River was highly respected among the Council of Elders. He frequently joined them in their meetings to share his visions and assist in any way possible to better the lives of his people. He had been feared by many of them as a child. His life essence had been granted by the river Spirit, imbuing him with great powers. No one knew his exact purpose, not even River himself. But their fears had all been for naught. The Spirit of the river was kind by nature and had no malevolence within it.

River headed towards the council house. It was a huge tree with silver leaves that stood at the center of the village. Two intricately carved doors opened to the hollowed area inside. The magic of the forest made the interior much larger than the tree outside would suggest. Most of the Elders had already gathered inside to discuss daily matters of life in the Vale.

"River, my friend." Brandor, a tall fair-haired elf, strode forward to greet him. "Welcome this fine morning," he said. "How are you?"

"I am well, Brandor, thank you. I have some news I wish to discuss with the council."

"You are always most welcome here, River, of course. Please be seated while I gather the others."

River sat at the oval-shaped table and waited. His mind swam with the images he had seen in the water. A heaviness weighed on the back of his mind, and he knew some work of evil was at hand.

The Elders each took their seats. "Good morning, gentle elves," Brandor said. "This morning we are joined by Lord River, who has come bearing some news for us." He gestured to River. "Go ahead, my friend."

"My lords, I have had a vision that troubles me greatly. I have seen savage creatures roaming in the Wildlands. They are unknown to me, and they have a sense of evil about them. They have not, as yet, attempted to cross the river, but I sense that they do not fear the magical barrier. I believe they are powered by some unknown magic of a very dark nature. I cannot see where they are from or where they have been, but I do feel strongly that they are a threat to us. I believe it's only a matter of time before they enter our lands." River's sapphire eyes were somber, his expression grave.

Silence filled the room with a heavy foreboding. The Vale had enjoyed many centuries of peace, and the thought of evil at its doorstep was difficult to digest. After a few moments, the Elders looked at one another. Finally, Rundil spoke. "My Lord River, will your magic be enough to protect our people from this menace?"

"For a while, I believe," River answered. "But some unknown source is giving power to these creatures. I might be able to determine what they are if I could see them up close. I'm not completely sure whether they aren't able to penetrate our magic or are choosing not to at this time. All I know is that the matter is most pressing. We must determine what this threat truly is."

The Elders began chattering amongst themselves just as the doors to the chamber flew open. "My Lords!" cried Rogin. "There is evil at work in our lands. A dryad was found badly beaten. She's been taken to my mother for healing."

Brandor spoke first. "This is indeed distressing news. A peaceful magical creature attacked near our very borders!" The room sounded with agreement and the anxious voices of the Elders.

"I must go to her," River said as he stood. "If these were the same creatures I saw in my vision, perhaps I can glean some evidence from her."

"I'll go with you, Father," Rogin said. River placed a hand on his shoulder and together they walked to the House of Medicine.

Inside, Lenora was ordering her maids to bring herbs to halt the bleeding. She was a highly skilled healer, but the dryad was severely wounded and near death. She looked up as River and her son entered. "I don't know if I can be of much help to her," she began. "This is savagery I have never seen. I fear her injuries will prove fatal. All I can do is try to make her passing as gentle as possible." Tears filled her eyes as she looked down at the beautiful creature lying before her. This was a peaceful fae of the forest. Harming a soul such as this was truly a most vile act.

River took her in his arms to comfort her, and she sobbed onto his shoulder. Dryads were indeed peaceful creatures who often assisted those who had lost their way in the forest. They were playful and good-natured and had no natural enemies.

Lenora wiped her eyes and stood back over the dryad. She laid her hands upon the dryad's heart and whispered words of comfort. White magic flowed through her fingertips and into the suffering form of the fae. Her face, formerly twisted in pain, changed to an expression of peace. She let out one final breath. Lenora whispered a prayer to the Goddess of the forest.

River knelt beside the lifeless dryad and laid his hand upon her forehead. He closed his eyes as blue magic spread over the dryad. Within seconds, her body disappeared. "She is at rest now," he said. "Her spirit is free. I have seen the creature who did this to her. I know now what it is we are facing." He looked into his life mate's eyes. "It is far worse than we could have imagined."

Chapter 4

Master Ulda stood at the coast, his black-red robe dancing behind him in the wind. He watched the black ships arriving from Ral'nassa and was pleased. His invasion could not have gone more smoothly. Sure, he had lost two assassins in his attempt to murder Al'marr's royal family, but the third attempt had succeeded. Men are so easily swayed by their love of gold that gaining inside help had been simple. Now Al'marr was his and so were its rich gem mines. Those gems would be the key to unlocking his unlimited power.

He held up a hand with his palm facing the ships. His impatience fueled the spell to move the ships along faster. They carried inside them the rest of his army. With them, he would have an easier time controlling his new subjects and quelling any rebellions that might be planned. The people of Al'marr would work for him, or they would die. He needed miners, polishers, and shapers for his gems. Naturally, he would still need farmers and bakers to provide food for the workers. It was not his desire to kill his own subjects. No, it would be much easier to kill citizens of the nearby kingdom of Na'zora. They were numerous and had provided him with several quality souls for binding.

Finally the ships made it to shore, and the soldiers began to disembark. Master Ulda turned to look at General Fru. "I trust you have assignments ready for these troops?"

General Fru replied, "Yes, your majesty. The plans are all in hand. Every inch of Al'marr will now be under watch by our troops. We should have extra to tend the mines and prevent any theft or halt of work."

"Excellent," Ulda replied. "Make sure they are aware that anyone caught stealing from me will face most dire consequences. I will deal with them personally."

"Yes, my lord." General Fru bowed and strode forward to meet his lieutenants.

Ulda turned and headed back up the slopes to his palace. It was small but suitable as a home for now.

After he had secured his place as absolute sovereign, he would begin work on a much more lavish home. By that time, he would be able to control the will of every subject in his realm.

He approached the palace doors as his servants rushed to open them. They bowed low as he walked through. First Minister Tu'vad was waiting for him in his throne room. Tu'vad had been an invaluable ally in Ulda's seizure of the throne. As First Minister to the former king, he had provided nearly every bit of information necessary for the murder of the royal family. He had personally opened the doors for Ulda's assassin. When the king's youngest daughter had tried to run, it was Tu'vad himself who grabbed her and snapped her neck.

"Majesty," Tu'vad said, bowing.

"Ah, Tu'vad," Ulda began "The rest of our army has arrived, and soon every corner of the kingdom will be fully under our control. I'm putting you in charge of the mines. They are of the utmost importance to me, so naturally I need someone in there I can trust. Make sure you install supervisors who are trustworthy as well. I cannot afford to lose a single gem. Ensure the largest gems are brought to the palace immediately. Have you taken care of the jewelers for me?"

"Yes, Majesty," Tu'vad replied. "Every jeweler in Al'marr has been brought to the palace, and a workshop has been set up on the lower floors. They are at your service, my king."

"You have done well again, Tu'vad. I shall not forget it. Do we have any new prisoners?"

"Today has been surprisingly quiet. I suspect word has gotten out of what happens to those who disobey their new king. Once the new troops are in place, I doubt you will have any trouble from the outlying villages for very long."

"We can always keep a few prisoners on hand, though." Ulda shook a finger at Tu'vad as he spoke. "You never know when we will need to use them."

Tu'vad nodded. "I'm sure there will be some petty thievery once the mines are running at full capacity. Even knowing the punishment, some people are always tempted to break the law."

"Very good. I don't want to run low on specimens." Ulda sat upon his stolen throne. If only those elves who were so keen to reject him could see him now. The ideas which caused him to be reviled by his peers in Ral'nassa were all coming into fruition now. He had managed all this with only a small group of soldiers and a few purses full of gold.

Humans were certainly much easier to conquer than elves. Had he tried to stage a coup in Ral'nassa, he would have had countless sorcerers to deal with. Surely some of them would have come to his side. Limitless power would be a very attractive reward for a sorcerer, but given the so-called morals of the royal council and the general dislike of dark wizardry, Ulda was sure to fail.

Here in Al'marr he had succeeded. Men are weak and their souls easily corrupted. They are easier to intimidate and not nearly as resistant to magic. Their so-called mages have to ingest regular potions just to cast the simplest spells. Without a doubt, Ulda would be able to persuade many human mages to assist him. He could offer them powers they had never imagined possible. All he would require is that they bend the knee to him.

Chapter 5

The drums summoned the clansmen to the feast.

The emissaries were seated next to the Overseer in a place of honor. Mel took a seat on the log bench next to Thinal, who already had a mouthful of honey cake. She swallowed the cake, gave Mel a guilty smile, and proceeded to lick her fingers. Mel smirked and shook his head.

The Overseer stood and raised a goblet. "These men here are emissaries from the king of Na'zora. They have come in peace to request our aid in a most urgent matter. Tonight, they are our honored guests, and tomorrow they will leave us."

Mel looked at Thinal, his jaw dropping open slightly. "Tomorrow?" he whispered.

Thinal smiled and shrugged.

"Eat, drink, make music, and dance!" the Overseer continued. "Tonight we feast!"

The clansmen responded with a cheer and began grabbing at the ample supply of food before them. Drums pounded, wooden flutes sang, and bones and shells rattled. A group of ladies began to dance. The shell bracelets on their ankles jingled and kept time with the music.

Despite the festivities, Mel was not fully at ease. He was not looking forward to working with these men from Na'zora. He didn't trust them and didn't want to work with them. He filled his plate with every kind of food available: fruits, nuts, boar meat, elk meat, and sweet cakes. Since he would be eating trail food for who knows how long, he was determined to enjoy a good meal tonight. The ale was in good supply as well. After a few mugs, he might be able to take his mind off the journey ahead.

One of the dancing ladies twirled by, bent down, and kissed Mel on the cheek. She offered a hand inviting him for a dance, but Mel shrugged and waved her away. Though their society was not particularly monogamous, he only had eyes for Thinal. She too was free to take other mates, but she seemed to prefer Mel above all others.

A group of fire twirlers took over the dance. They each held flaming wooden batons which they tossed back and forth and threw high into the sky. Applause roared from the gathered elves. The twirlers took a bow, doused their flames, and began dancing with the ladies. The music swelled louder, and many elves from the crowd joined in the dance.

Thinal, who had just downed a mug of ale, grabbed Mel by the arm and dragged him to the dance area. He still had a mouthful of food, but he swallowed, smiled, and began dancing. Thinal's eyes twinkled with starlight, and she smiled and laughed as they danced. For the moment, Mel forgot his troubles and focused only on his lover.

After several dances, the pair sank back into their seats and reached for more ale. They touched glasses and drank. Once his cup was emptied, Mel stretched out on the log bench and focused his green eyes up at the stars. Thinal, mug in hand, asked, "What do you see up there?" She smiled as she gazed up into the heavens.

After a pause, Mel replied, "The future and the past." He sighed and added, "Everything." With another sigh, he sat up and looked at Thinal. She set down her mug, took his hands, and looked up towards the sky.

"I think I see it too," she said with a smile.

"Pardon me," a voice said. "I don't wish to interrupt."

They looked and saw Mi'tal standing next to them. He took a seat on the log next to Mel.

"Perhaps this isn't the best time, but I would like to say a few words to you both. I know my people have not always treated you kindly. There is tension between us because of the past, but I do not believe we are the same as we once were. King Aelryk is older and far wiser than he used to be. He is no longer a young prince under the orders of his father. In his youth, he was eager to prove himself a true leader in battle. He followed his father's orders without question. Many years have passed since then, and I do believe his views have changed. He enjoys the peace we share with your people. I truly believe that in time he will do all he can to make amends."

Mel was silent, contemplative.

"The war was a long time ago," Thinal said. "Neither of us had been born yet. Our parents fought in it along with some of the elder members of our clan, but I think you have a chance for a fresh start with the youth. It's true our numbers are growing, and in time we will need more space. I hope you will allow us an audience with your king, and I hope he will listen. Personally, I am helping you because I want to see what lies beyond our borders. I also wouldn't mind the chance to take on a few of these monsters of yours." Her lips turned up into a mischievous smile.

"You may not wish that once you've seen them, my lady, but you are indeed brave," Mi'tal said. "It will be an honor to have you and your sword along on this journey."

Mel remained silent. He was listening to every word, but he had nothing to say. Perhaps this man was telling the truth, and perhaps this king had grown wiser over the years. Thinal was going, so he must go. She was willing to trust these men, and Mel trusted her judgment.

Mi'tal rose. "I suppose I will see you both in the morning then." He nodded at Mel and walked away.

The festivities continued late into the night, and finally Mel and Thinal headed for their hut. Once inside, Thinal undressed and washed her face. She pulled the shell comb from her hair allowing the dark tresses to fall freely. Mel lay flat on the bed, exhausted. Thinal, however, was still swimming with excitement.

"I can't wait to get started!" she said. "This is a chance to wander farther into the Wildlands than any of us has ever been. Maybe they'll even let us explore part of Na'zora. Just imagine being allowed to wander freely in their lands. What if their king actually granted your request? That would mean so much to our people."

She sat on the edge of the bed and put her hand on Mel's shoulder. "I know you're going to hate these men and any others we have to deal with, but promise me you'll see it through to the end. Promise me, Mel."

"I promise," Mel said. He closed his eyes and slept.

Chapter 6

"You will not win this war without the river! There is a war coming. I have seen it. I cannot change a prophecy for anyone. Not even for you, your Majesty." Orzi stood with his back bent and his fists pressing hard upon the table. He was clearly exhausted. His apprentice helped ease him back into his seat.

"I wish you would make your prophecy more clear," King Aelryk said with a sigh. "I have three mages, four historians, and every scholar at the college looking into this. No one has discovered anything useful. There simply aren't any lands of spring. I fear it is hopeless."

Orzi closed his eyes. It was always the same with kings. They wanted every prophecy to be specific and tell them exactly what to do. That just isn't how prophecy works. Why couldn't they realize that if he could be specific he would do it? He wished he could always tell them exactly how to make things right. It just wasn't that easy.

"My king, I have told you everything that I can. I will keep trying to see more, but for now that is all I see. An evil is gathering and you need the river."

"That raises another question that I haven't wanted to consider just yet. How am I supposed to bring a river back with me? Do I have to move the entire river, or can I bring some back in a jar?" Aelryk changed to a gentler tone. "Orzi, I know you are doing everything you can to help. I hope you can understand my frustration. Lives are at stake. I only wish to protect my people."

* * * * *

The king had just sat down for dinner when a page burst through the door.

"Your majesty, sir," the out-of-breath page said as he kneeled on one knee. "Magister Utric has found an answer to your riddle, umm, prophecy, sir. He is gathering his documents and said you can expect him straight away." The page was still breathing heavily. Obviously, he had run to the king's chambers all the way from the Tower of Learning.

"Thank you for this information, young man. You may go." Aelryk motioned at his cupbearer to pour him some wine. His appetite had been waning but his thirst had not. He sipped at the wine impatiently.

Once again the door opened, and Aelryk looked up anticipating the magister. However, it was Queen Lisalla who entered the dining room followed closely by her maid.

"Good evening, my lady," Aelryk said, standing. As she approached, he reached out for her hand and kissed it.

"Good evening, my lord," she replied as she took a seat at the table. Quickly, the king's cupbearer poured her a glass of wine. She sipped the wine and asked, "Is there any news? I saw the page running in your direction."

"Yes, I believe there is. I'm just waiting for Magister Utric to make his way here. Supposedly, he has figured out where it is I need to go. With any luck, he has also figured out what it is I need to do."

"It's a long walk from the tower, dear. Perhaps we should go ahead and eat." She motioned the servants to bring their dinner. Right away, each of them had a small hen and vegetables placed before them. The queen proceeded to eat, but Aelryk was preoccupied in thought. He sipped at another glass of wine and tapped a finger against the surface of the table.

Finally, Magister Utric arrived accompanied by his apprentice. Both men carried books and scrolls in their arms. "Forgive me, your majesty, for interrupting your meal. I thought you would like to know what I have found immediately."

"Indeed," Aelryk said. "Tell me what it is you've found."

"Of course, majesty. I have found these ancient documents stashed away. I believe they were somehow spared from the great fire that destroyed the Tower of Learning around four hundred years ago. They tell of a land of eternal spring and of a long forgotten group of elves who lived in the area. I believe, based on the description of its location, that it is within the Westerling Vale. The Blue River flows through it and actually has its source in the mountains just above the Vale."

"You're certain about this?" Queen Lisalla asked. "That is quite a long way to travel."

"Yes, my lady, I am quite certain. I will of course confer with the other historians, but I didn't want to hesitate to inform his majesty."

"Thank you, magister. Please gather the others immediately to discuss this finding. Send for Orzi as well." King Aelryk felt relieved. In his heart, he knew that this was the answer. To the fabled land of the Westerling Elves was where he would be traveling. As a child he had heard tales of them, but they were surely just a myth. These were elves out of legend that had not been seen by any man now living.

Chapter 7

Hammers rang in the darkness as sparkling gems were pulled from the earth. The miners worked without speaking. If the guards caught them chatting during work hours, they were beaten. Those who dropped from exhaustion were taken away and not seen again. Rumors began to spread through the camps that they were being used for experimentation. Some said they were being transformed into monsters. Others said they were being drained of their life essence and used to power dark magic. Whatever the case, the miners preferred not to find out firsthand.

Tu'vad inspected the tables which were covered with small dark gems. Some of them were so small that they would be completely useless once they were cut into the proper shape. Many, however, were large enough to suit his master's needs. Unfortunately, none had yet been discovered that warranted immediate attention. Master Ulda would need some very large gems as well, but they were quite rare.

Tu'vad would simply force the workers to dig deeper and deeper and provide them fewer hours of sleep. That should speed up the process and make his master happy. Tu'vad would not be blamed for the lack of larger gems as long as he was pushing the workers to their limits. Three mines were currently in operation, so with a little luck, larger gems would start turning up soon.

Two female workers began clearing the tables. They sorted the gems by size and placed them in chests. The tiny ones, no doubt, would be ground into dust and used for medicinal purposes. At least, that was their traditional use in Al'marr. The medium sized ones were formerly used for jewelry, but they would soon hold the source of power for Master Ulda's enchantments.

The ladies loaded the chests into carts which would then be taken to the gem cutters. Each gem would be cut and polished to Ulda's precise specifications. The facets had to be just right for the magic to work. A few of the gem cutters had already provided Ulda with perfectly cut gems, and Tu'vad hoped the new cutters would do the same. If not, they wouldn't be given another chance to fail. He would see to them personally.

"Guards," Tu'vad called. Two guards appeared immediately at his side. "Escort these women and their carts to the jewelers at the palace."

"Yes, my lord," one guard replied, and both of them obeyed at once.

Tu'vad walked over to inspect the mining camp. The overnight workers were either sleeping or having a bite to eat. Tu'vad wanted to inspect the food to be sure they weren't overeating. The cook was stirring a stew over the fire as Tu'vad approached. "A heavy stomach makes for a lazy worker," Tu'vad said. "Add some more water to that stew and only issue half-size slices of bread."

"But sir, the workers aren't eating enough as is!" the skinny cook protested.

Tu'vad immediately grabbed his throat and pressed his knife under the man's chin. "No one talks back to me. If they do, they die or worse. I'm going to excuse you this once. Disobey me again, and you will have my promise fulfilled."

He released the shaken cook and proceeded towards the camp guards.

"I want every tent searched daily for stolen gems. Anyone caught stealing is to be bound and dragged to the palace dungeons."

"As you command, my lord," one of the guards said.

Tu'vad decided that being in charge of the mines wasn't so bad. He would continue to prove useful to Master Ulda, and in time, he would be the richest man in Al'marr. Power was well and good, but he didn't want the responsibility of running the entire nation. Ulda could have that. Tu'vad wanted gold, land, women, and servants to obey him when he spoke. His life could only get better from here.

* * * * *

Ulda stood over a large metal table with an orb in the center. What had once been the king's sitting room was now Ulda's laboratory. Here he could create enchantments much stronger than any carved runes. Runes had their purpose, but with the gems and essences of his victims, Ulda's powers of enchantment had greatly increased.

Extracting the essences of humans is rather easy. Their souls are young and separated from the world around them because they have very little connection with the earth. However, if Ulda could successfully bind the spirits of elves, he would be unstoppable. An elven essence could power frighteningly strong enchantments, but those experiments would have to wait. He had not yet perfected his technique to extract the essence of elves.

There were stories of Telorithan, a sorcerer from the Sunswept Isles, who had managed to bind the essence of a fire spirit. No other living being had ever managed to bind an elemental. Ulda wasn't sure if the stories could possibly be true. If they were, this sorcerer would have immense power. Perhaps someday Ulda would learn from him.

At this point, he was content using human essences. The power he derived from them could be the key to collecting the more powerful souls of elves. That was his goal for now.

A knock came from his door. "Master Ulda, my lord," a voice said from the other side. "I bring freshly cut and polished gems for you, sir."

"Enter," Ulda said.

An old man carrying a wooden chest entered the room. He kept his head bowed and awaited instructions.

"Lay it there on the table and leave," Ulda said, pointing at the table in the far corner.

The old man bowed, placed the chest on the table, and turned to leave.

"Wait," Ulda commanded.

The old man froze and turned to face him.

"Have you been a jeweler all of your life?" Ulda asked.

"Yes, majesty. I have shaped stones since I was a very young man."

"Excellent," Ulda said. "You can personally inspect all of the gems before they're brought to me. It is tedious work that I don't have time for myself. I will trust you to do this, and if I find any problems, I'll know who to punish. You're dismissed."

"Yes, sir. Thank you." The old man bowed again and left the room.

The old man was afraid of him, and that gave Ulda pleasure. Fear is a powerful emotion and seems to make a human consciousness easier to bind. Torment works well too. If he left a victim in agony before extracting their essence, the work seemed to go much easier. This bit of knowledge might help him graduate to binding elves. Elves, however, are not easily made afraid, and they can withstand greater amounts of physical pain. On the other hand, mental anguish works just as well, and elven peoples tend to feel more deeply for the things around them.

That did not apply to all elves, of course, as Ulda himself could care less for others. He preferred being left alone to his studies and had little use for companionship. The humans and elves around him served their intended purposes, and he required no more from them. Among his kind, the Enlightened Elves, friendship was not necessary. Knowledge of the arcane sciences was prized above all else. Ulda's intention was to become the most knowledgeable and powerful sorcerer of them all.

Chapter 8

"Adda!" young Alyra shouted as she ran down the hill towards her father.

"Hello there, my sweet," River said as the little girl reached him.

She threw her arms around him and squeezed tightly. After a moment, she released him and sat on the intricately carved bench next to him. Here, under the boughs of a weeping willow, was River's favorite place to sit and think. Within the gardens near his home that overlook the Blue River, he would peacefully sit for many hours.

Alyra, his youngest daughter, was a beautiful dark-haired child with features similar to her father's. Her blue dress was dirty at the hem, most likely due to some make believe adventure. Escaping from her lessons had become a hobby of hers. She liked to sneak away and make the short, but epic in her mind, journey to sit with her father beneath the willow tree.

"What did you learn today, little one?" River asked.

"I learned that when Miss Hilla is reading histories aloud, she doesn't look up in time to see me sneak away."

River smiled.

Silently, they sat together in the beautiful spring weather of the Vale. Birds sang, and the wind blew softly through the trees. The river rushed softly along, filling the air with the scent of water.

Afternoon wore on and Lenora entered the gardens to find her life mate and youngest child. Alyra waved cheerily as she saw her mother approach. She stopped waving, and a guilty look came across her face as she saw Miss Hilla following closely behind her mother.

"There you are, my sneaky child," Miss Hilla said. Her kind eyes danced as she looked at the girl. It was impossible to be angry with the child just for showing spirit.

"Alyra, you owe Miss Hilla an apology for sneaking away. It was very impolite," Lenora said. "Now go with her and finish up your lessons for the day."

Alyra stood and started walking towards Hilla. Suddenly, she stopped, turned on her heels, and ran back to River. She hugged him tightly, and he kissed her forehead. He smiled as she walked away with Hilla.

As he stood, he kissed his life mate's hand and asked, "Shall we walk in the gardens, my love?"

"I'd love to," she replied, taking him by the arm.

Together they strolled along the path leading through the gardens. Blue, purple, and yellow flowers bloomed all along the path. Trees covered with white and pink flowers swayed softly in the breeze. The air was filled with the intoxicating mix of these fragrant blossoms. Yellow butterflies fluttered lazily on the wind.

"Tell me, my dear," Lenora said. "Has there been any news of the intruders in the woodlands?"

"Rogin and his troops have increased patrols. They are searching further into the forest than usual. Some strange tracks have also been seen, but no other sign of the creatures has been found. Still, we must be vigilant."

They took a path leading off to the left and down to the river. Lenora sat on a bench overlooking the water. River knelt in front of her.

"Lenora, my love, the attack on the dryad was not the work of a naturally occurring creature. Some dark magic has conjured them and is using them for an evil purpose. Through my visions, I have seen that it was an attempt to trap her essence. The creature wanted to kidnap her, not kill her. She fought much too strongly to allow herself to be carried away."

Lenora sat silent, stunned. Her eyes widened and she took a deep breath. Her golden hair blew gently in the breeze. After a moment, she spoke. "Is it possible to bind a dryad's essence? And what could someone do with it if they succeeded?"

"I do not truly know. Dryads are born of the woods themselves. It would be like binding the essence of a tree. I'm not sure it is possible, but if someone is trying with creatures...," he broke off and looked at the ground.

"They are most likely planning to try with people too," Lenora finished. "Or perhaps they are already doing such a thing."

"I fear these new creatures have been conjured by binding the essences of men," River said. "I know of no other way to create a new species. This is very powerful magic, and the world of men will not know how to combat it."

"Do you think they will come looking for us? It's been centuries since we have had any contact with them."

"I have seen it, my love. They will come. They need us."

"Well," Lenora said. "Let's hope they treat us better than they do the Young Ones. I'm not inclined to trust them, and I am glad your magic has kept them away so long. Our people are better for it."

"Nevertheless, I know they cannot defeat this enemy alone. If they were to fall, this evil would spread to us next. I do not know if my magic could keep it away. I do not know what we are facing."

"Let's sit a while and forget these troubles, dear," she said as she patted the bench next to her.

River took a seat and wrapped his arm around her shoulders. She leaned her golden head on his chest and closed her eyes.

Chapter 9

Morning arrived and Mel and Thinal were ready to head out. The summer air was mild, and the sun's rays shone softly through the trees above. They stood at the edge of their village facing north into the dense forest.

"If they're late, I'm going back to bed, " Mel said.

He looked over his shoulder and saw Loren, Mi'tal, and their two guards heading down the path.

"Damn," Mel said with a sigh.

Thinal smiled at him and adjusted the scabbard on her back which held her two-handed sword. She slung her cross-body sack over her left shoulder, making sure the strap was clear of her sword. She did not expect to have need of the blade anytime soon, but she liked to be prepared in any case.

"I could pick them off from here," Mel said, holding his bow.

The pair laughed. Mel stared impatiently as the group approached.

"Good morning to you both," Mi'tal said. "I don't believe you've met Byord and Oli." He gestured to the two guards. They nodded, Thinal smiled, and Mel stared at them blankly.

"There's no chance you'll let us bring our horses?" Loren asked.

"The lady can share mine," Byord said, a broad grin appearing on his face.

"Remind me to punch you in the throat later," Mel said. "Tracking from a horse in these woods is nearly impossible. You'll miss half the signs and trample over the rest. Do whatever the hell you want with your horses. I'm going on foot."

"We have stabled our horses, and they will be well looked after here with your clansmen," Mi'tal replied. "My friend Loren is a bit overweight, but he will manage the walk."

Loren looked annoyed but remained silent.

"Let's get to it then," Thinal said as she turned and headed out into the woods.

"I would like to head to the border village of Enald. There may be some news of the creatures there," Mi'tal said.

"I know the village," Mel replied. "We've traded there for many years. It's only about a day and a half walk from here. No one has gone that way for weeks, so any strange tracks should be easy to spot."

"Thank you," Mi'tal said. "How do you find the trading at Enald?"

"The people are fair. We usually bring leathers, furs, and nuts. Some of my clansmen trade trinkets, crafts, and bone tools."

"Mel likes to trade for spices," Thinal broke in. "He likes the hot ones." Smiling, she nudged him with her elbow.

"Yes, I do, and I'm not interested in their tobacco or jewels," Mel looked at her and smiled. "Or in their sweets."

"I also like their pretty cloth," Thinal said. "They always have very pretty hair trinkets too, but they're just a bit too delicate for me."

Mel stopped walking and pointed to a small broken branch. "A deer passed this way about an hour ago. He would have been good for dinner, but he's headed west, not north."

They walked on throughout the morning. Just after mid-day, they came upon a small clearing.

"Might we stop a moment and have a bite to eat?" Loren asked.

"Seems like a good place," Thinal said as she removed her bag and sat on a fallen log. She reached into the bag and brought out a handful of dry seeds. She popped one in her mouth and offered them to Mel. He took one, chewed it, and stood up.

"I'll find some things to eat," he said as he headed off.

Oli removed his rucksack and opened it. Inside was hard bread and cheese. He passed these items out to his companions who began munching hungrily. Only Thinal was uninterested and graciously declined. She sat chewing on seeds until Mel returned. He was carrying a large leaf filled with berries, roots, and a few leaves.

"Well, this looks delicious," Byord said sarcastically.

"Shove it," Mel said. "Next time I'll bring you a special surprise." He smiled a wicked smile and set the provisions on a stump. "There's plenty for everyone else."

Mi'tal reached over and took a few berries. He smelled them first and then gave one a try. "These are very good!" he said without hiding his surprise. He grabbed a root and crunched it. "Not as flavorful, but it's quite filling. Have some," he gestured to the others who slowly took a few pieces of food.

"The roots will settle your stomach if the berries are too rich," Thinal said.

"Are the leaves for wiping our asses?" Byord said, laughing.

"They're for cleaning your teeth afterwards," Mel replied. "Unless you want to walk around like a purple-mouthed idiot. The purple would be a change for you at least."

"Byord, don't speak for the rest of the journey," Mi'tal said. "I tire of your childishness."

Byord rolled his eyes but remained silent. Mi'tal was his commander, and he would obey whether he liked it or not.

"This is delightful, Mel. Thank you for bringing this to us," Mi'tal said as he finished eating. He looked over at Loren who was greedily licking his plump fingers.

They sat a few moments more and then continued on their way. The break was short but very welcome. The day had grown warmer, and the dense forest air was moist. A gentle breeze rustled the green leaves around them. All was silent except for the lazy whistle of a yellow bird.

On they walked through the afternoon until Mel silently held up a hand for them to stop. He looked to his right and still remained silent. Suddenly, they heard a loud *thwack*. Mel had drawn his bow and shot a squirrel on the ground. Mi'tal jumped, startled by the sound. He was standing next to Mel but had neither seen him grab his bow nor knock an arrow.

Mel looked at him and said, "One."

Thinal took a step forward and nudged Mel with her elbow. She pointed up in one of the trees.

Thwack! Another squirrel fell from above.

"Two," Mel said to Mi'tal and smiled.

Mel gathered the two squirrels and removed their guts. Then, he hung them from his belt by their tails. Loren's expression was one of disgust. Tonight would be his first dinner that included rodent.

Mel noticed his expression and said, "They're really good. Maybe we can catch a few more."

Thinal giggled, and the group began moving again. Along the way, she picked a small blue flower and tucked it behind her ear. Her movements were light and playful as if she had never had a care in the world. She bent slightly to kiss her mate on his cheek. He smiled back and grabbed a white flower which he offered to her. She took it and quickly popped it in her mouth. Those flowers had a particularly sweet, honey-like taste, which had always been her favorite.

Evening approached and the group began looking for a place to bed down for the night. Mel had managed to catch two more squirrels which meant there was plenty of food to go around. A few wild herbs would set the meat off nicely.

Mel led them to a copse of trees on a small hill. This was a good location to stay the night. The trees were tall and wide and strong enough to hold them all.

"We'll camp here tonight," Mel said, loosening his quiver and setting it at the base of the largest tree. "I'll build a fire and get dinner started."

Thinal removed her scabbard and set it next to Mel's quiver. She pulled the bone pin from her hair and shook her head side to side. After running her fingers through her hair a few times, she rose to search for some herbs. Mel already had the fire started and was removing the fur from the squirrels.

The men unpacked their bedrolls and laid them on the ground.

"The trees are safer," Mel said, still skinning a squirrel.

"Safer for what?" Loren asked.

"Safer for sleeping," Mel replied. "No dangerous animal in these woods can climb trees."

"Well, we prefer the ground," Loren said snobbishly.

"Suit yourself," Mel shrugged. "If I hear screaming in the night, I'll know to stay in the trees."

Thinal returned and handed Mel some herbs she had found. He rubbed them into the meat and skewered it before placing it over the flames. He moved back to sit next to Thinal and took a sip from his waterskin.

"Dinner smells lovely," she said. "Too bad there are no evergreens near. Some pine needle tea would go lovely with it."

"When we get to Enald you can have some of that blended tea that you like so much," he said.

"Oh, I had forgotten about that," she said with a smile.

Mel went over to check on the meat. It had cooked thoroughly and was giving off a pleasant aroma. He pulled it into pieces and laid it on the rocks nearby. "Eat up," he said as he grabbed some for himself and Thinal. She sat next to him and took a piece of the meat. Tasting it, she nodded her approval.

Mi'tal ate before the others would try it. Once he had tasted it, they felt safe to have some as well. Loren, however, still refused to touch the food. He would only eat the bread and cheese they had brought from their homeland.

"You really should have some, Loren," Mi'tal said. "It's insulting to our host to refuse his generosity. It may not be what you're accustomed to, but it's quite good."

Loren scowled and chomped on the tough bread in his mouth.

"No worries," Thinal smiled. "It leaves more for the rest of us."

"You're always so upbeat, Miss Thinal," Mi'tal said. "It's very refreshing to see someone so carefree and truly happy."

"I just don't see any reason to be unhappy," she said, shrugging. "Some people sit and worry, but I don't. I just go with it. You might as well try to make the best of every situation. Sulking isn't any fun anyway."

"Sulking is my job," Mel said. "I'll sit in the rain, and you can stand in the sunshine."

"Aww," Thinal said and rubbed his shoulder. "My poor sweet Mel. He worries enough for both of us."

He rolled his eyes and looked at the ground. She ran her fingers through his sandy hair and kissed his lips. Wrapping an arm around his neck, she pulled him in close. He nestled his face in the curve of her neck.

"Anyone up for a game?" Oli asked producing a deck of cards.

Thinal jumped up, startling Mel. "I'd love to play if you'll teach me," she said.

"Then have a seat here, my lady," Oli said as he took a seat cross-legged behind a stump.

Mel watched her walk away and then looked over at Mi'tal, who was rubbing a cloth along his war hammer. "Why do you carry a hammer instead of a sword?" Mel asked, moving to sit next to Mi'tal.

"Better for smashing heads," he replied, laughing.

Mel laughed as well and nodded. "Most of your kinsmen carry swords, though. I've only heard of dwarves fighting with hammers."

"Axes too, if I'm not mistaken," Mi'tal said. "But I've never encountered a dwarf myself. My father used a war hammer, and he taught me. I studied swordplay a few years in my youth, but I never really took to it. Hammers are slower, but they're very efficient in a fight."

"Did you fight in the War of the Wildlands?" Mel asked.

"I did," Mi'tal replied. "I was in King Aelryk's personal guard. Though, he was Prince Aelryk at that time."

"Did you kill many of my kind?" Mel looked him in the eye.

After a pause, Mi'tal said, "A few. To my shame they were mostly women. I was never within range of any of your archers, but I encountered your swordswomen on a few occasions. They are formidable opponents and even more so when they're fighting for their homeland."

He looked at Mel and drew a deep breath. Mel looked away and remained silent.

"I have many regrets from that war," Mi'tal admitted. "I followed my king's command, but in my heart I knew it was unjust. We could have lived together in peace. I'm sure of it."

"The wars ended just a few years before I was born," Mel said. "I've heard many stories, of course, but never one from the enemy's side. I would agree my people did some less than honorable things in those times, but most of our actions were justified, I think."

"After staying a few days with your clan I'd say you've made the best of a difficult situation. Your people have thrived in the Forests of Viera."

"We have, but there is little room to grow. I don't take to strangers easily, Mi'tal, but I think you are as honorable a man as I have met."

"Thank you, Mel," Mi'tal replied. "I know very few Wild Elves myself, but I find you honest and respectable."

Mel nodded and turned to watch Thinal playing at her card game. She had won another hand and gave a little clap. Yawning, she stretched her arms high over her head. She stood and walked back to Mel.

"Ready for bed?" she asked.

Nodding, he stood and took her hand. With a boost from Mel, she climbed up in the tallest tree and settled on a wide branch. He followed closely behind her. The sounds of their love making filled the camp as the others settled into their bedrolls.

* * * * *

Dawn broke, and a breakfast of nuts and berries already awaited the men who had slept on the ground. Mel and Thinal were ready to head out, but they waited as the others had their breakfast and packed up their gear.

"We'll be at Enald by this afternoon," Mel said. "That is if we ever get moving again." Finally, the group was ready to set out again, and they walked noisily through the woods.

"Why don't we walk a little bit louder!" Mel shouted, obviously annoyed.

"Who cares about the noise," Loren said. "We aren't hunting."

"No," Mel replied, "but something may be hunting us."

The men began to tread more lightly after that. They had all seen firsthand the work of these dark creatures, and they did not enjoy the thought they may be nearby. They traveled all morning and straight through mid-day to reach Enald as quickly as possible.

Finally, the village came into view, and the Na'zorans were relieved to see it. It was a small market village at the border of their country, and the bustle observed from a distance suggested business as usual. There were no signs of an attack by the monsters.

Upon arrival, Mi'tal was immediately recognized by a courier. The courier had been drinking at an outdoor tavern and slammed his mug down on the table. He ran to Mi'tal, wiping his mouth with his sleeve.

"My lord, Mi'tal," he hiccupped. "I've been waiting for you, sir, to bring you a message from the king. He requests that you and the elves you've employed meet him up north at Duana. You'll be traveling to the Westerling Vale."

"The Vale?!" Mel exclaimed angrily.

"The Vale!" Thinal echoed excitedly. "Can you believe it? I've heard so many stories of the Vale!"

"Bedtime stories," Mel said sharply. "The place is a myth. It's the make believe home of Mistonwey, God of the Rivers." Mel shook his head and sighed. Convincing Thinal not to go to a land of myth would be harder than chopping down a tree with his teeth.

"Why the Vale?" Mi'tal asked the courier.

"No idea, sir. I'm just supposed to make sure you head that way immediately. Horses are available for you at the livery."

"Thank you, young man. Please get a message to the king that we are on our way." Mi'tal flipped him a coin and turned to face Mel and Thinal. "I hope this isn't too much of an inconvenience for you. I know this wasn't what you expected, but there must be some pressing matter regarding the Vale. Perhaps that's where the creatures are coming from."

Mel sighed, and the group followed Mi'tal towards the stables. "We'll be needing horses for six," he told the stable hand.

"And a pony for my little friend here," Byord added and patted Mel on the head. Mel, who had had enough of Byord's stupidity, quickly turned and punched him in the crotch. Byord doubled over and moaned.

"That was hardly worth it, was it?" Mi'tal said. "Six horses, please. We're going to have some lunch, and I will expect them to be ready when we've finished."

"Yes sir, my lord," the stable hand said and went off to tend the horses.

The six of them headed along the dirt road to the inn for a quick bite to eat. The food was hot, and the ale was dark. Thinal asked for a glass of tea and was delighted when it arrived. Mel downed two mugs of ale and belched at Byord.

Once they had finished eating and drinking, they headed back to the stables. Six brown horses were saddled and ready to go.

"To Duana, then," Loren said as he mounted one of the horses.

"It's only about a day's ride along the road from here," Mi'tal told the elves.

"Let's get going," Mel said, offering Thinal a hand as she mounted her horse. He hopped up on the horse next to hers, and the group set out riding north.

Chapter 10

"Twit!" Ulda shouted as he slapped the young elf across his face. "I asked for skilled sorcerers to join me, not inept morons!" The young elf cowered in fear. "If you can't learn these skills, then I'll use you for a test subject."

"Please, master," the young elf pleaded. "I will try harder."

Ulda took a deep breath and let it out slowly. Apparently training his special force of Soulbinders would be more difficult than he had anticipated. Still, he was going to need their help, so he would have to learn some patience.

"Look, all of you," he turned to face his group of twenty-five sorcerers. "You are some of the finest sorcerers of Ral'nassa. You have joined me for a very special purpose, and you must pay close attention to these lessons. The slightest lapse in concentration will cause the binding to fail and destroy the gem. We have very few of them to waste, so I expect you to work hard."

He motioned to the skinny young boy standing at the door. "Slave, sit here on the floor." He pointed to the center of the room in front of the sorcerers. "You there," he said, pointing to a dark-haired sorcerer in a red robe. "Bind this one. Use his fear."

The sorcerer stepped forward, his palms raised facing the boy. With his thumb and forefinger, he held a small purple gem. A deep purple glow began to materialize on his hands as he adjusted the angle of the gem. Suddenly, a beam of purple light shot from the sorcerer, through the gem, and into the boy's chest. The boy screamed with fright and was slowly lifted off his feet. He threw back his head, and his entire body jerked wildly. As quickly as it had begun, it was over. The magic faded and the boy dropped lifelessly to the floor.

The sorcerer held the gem high and inspected the pale light swirling within it. He turned and held the gem out for his colleagues to observe.

Ulda applauded the student. "Well done! That is exactly the process I am trying to teach you. The next step is using this essence to power other enchantments."

He walked to the door, opened it, and called to someone outside. A few moments later, a cage containing a large spotted wildcat was wheeled in. Its yellow eyes scanned the elves present in the room.

"I'm sure you all recognize one of Ral'nassa's beautiful wildcats. I've had enough brought over for each of you. Using a human consciousness to power the enchantment, you can turn this savage beast into a most impressive mount. They are sturdy, swift, and will fight fiercely on your behalf. I will demonstrate."

Ulda went behind the caged animal and plucked a few hairs from its tail. The cat swatted and hissed at the sorcerer. A smile spread across Ulda's face as he inspected the hairs closely.

"Shed hairs do not work as well since they rarely contain a living cell. Plucked hairs work quite nicely for this next step. Follow me." He led his students to the large metal table with the orb at the center. As he touched his hand to the orb, it began to spin. Gently, he placed the hairs inside.

"Your gem, master Soulbinder," Ulda said as he extended his hand. The sorcerer in red quickly handed over the filled gem. Ulda placed the gem inside the orb and placed both hands just above it as a purple glow filled the sphere. In a blinding flash of light, the gem burst, and the light shot out into Ulda's fingertips. He turned towards the cat and fired the magic towards it, hitting it full in the face.

"This cat is now yours, Soulbinder," Ulda said, smiling proudly at his student.

The students stood in awe of this new magic. It was unlike anything they had seen before. Such power was unheard of using the magic they were taught at the college.

The red-robed sorcerer walked boldly up to the caged wildcat and released the latch on its door. The cat walked out calmly and licked his hand. Purring softly, it proceeded to rub its face all over the laughing elf.

"Marvelous," he said. "Simply, marvelous." He stroked the cat's head and neck as it stretched and purred.

"The rest of you must practice until you have mastered the binding. Later, I will show you how to combine the essence of a beast with the essence of a man, creating a new creature in the process. For now, practice on the slaves I've provided, and try not to waste them. I don't have many disposable citizens yet. Not until we've taken Na'zora."

Ulda strode out of the room leaving his pupils behind to master this new art. He was certain they would pick it up quickly. They were eager to learn and to succeed.

The stone corridor echoed with his footsteps as he headed towards his throne room. Tapestries had been hung by his command along all the walls. They featured colors from all the schools of magic except for white. Ulda did not care for the healing arts. They were a waste of his valuable time. Mystical bindings had always been his strong suit, and he was pleased to be bringing them to a whole new level.

The servants within bowed low as he entered the throne room. Ignoring them, he perched himself upon the dark blue cushion which had been crafted to mold to his body. He propped his feet upon a low stool and let his arms dangle over the sides of his throne.

Tu'vad entered, stood before the throne, and bowed.

"How are the mines coming along?" Ulda asked.

"Nicely, your majesty," Tu'vad replied. "Miners are working around the clock in two shifts. They are finding some larger gems than before, but no very large stones have been found just yet. We will continue working."

"Very well," Ulda said, bored with the news. If he wanted to create stronger enchantments, he would need larger gems. Waiting drove him mad, but there wasn't much else he could do. He trusted that Tu'vad was pushing the miners as hard as possible without killing them. Disgusting creatures that they were, Ulda needed their labor. At least he didn't have to look at them often.

"You may go, Tu'vad," Ulda said, waving his hand. "Send General Fru in. We need to discuss future plans."

"Right away, highness," Tu'vad bowed and took three steps backwards before leaving the room.

Ulda sat idly staring up at the ceiling, his fingers interlaced across his chest. Training his students this morning had been exhausting work. They were all masters of arcane knowledge, but they lacked discipline. They were arrogant and set in their ways despite being rather young. Still, they were eager to learn what he could teach them. Unlimited power was quite a tantalizing lure for a young sorcerer. Naturally, he would not teach them everything. Should one of them try to overpower him, he would need the few tricks he was holding back. He would not be overthrown.

Finally, General Fru arrived in the throne room and bowed.

"Ah, General," Ulda said, sitting up in his seat. "We need to discuss plans for our future invasion of Na'zora. My students are learning quickly and will soon be able to create more of our wolf-man hybrids. We're going to need Na'zora's supply of souls if we are ever to take over Ral'nassa. We should also consider attacking those pesky Wild Elves. I can't imagine their essences being much more difficult to bind than a human. Enlightened Elves, however, are going to prove a much greater challenge."

"The weaponsmiths are working overtime to create the finest swords and armor possible for our troops. Will your Soulbinders be able to place enchantments on the blades, or will we need a rune carver?"

"Enchanting a weapon is a mere trifle," Ulda said. "Minor ones can be done with only the essence of an animal. Rune carving is well and good, but the enchantments created using a soul are much stronger and more efficient. Have you appointed anyone to work with the spiderlings yet?"

"Yes, sir," Fru replied. "They will be grown in a few days and ready for your use."

"Excellent. I'm most excited to see this new hybrid," Ulda said. "My Soulbinders should be up to the task by then."

"Is there anything else you need from me, sire?" Fru asked.

"Not at this time. You may go."

General Fru bowed and left the room. Ulda relaxed back into his chair and sighed. Things were coming along nicely. Within a year or two, he could be the king of all Nōl'Deron. The thought brought a smile to his face as he closed his eyes and drifted to sleep.

Chapter 11

"Your highness, I beg you," Magister Utric pleaded. "I know I am old and will only be in the way, but I must accompany you. If indeed these elves still live in the Vale, I must document them. There are so many things we might learn from them."

"This is not a scholarly mission, Magister," Aelryk replied. "We will be traveling through some dangerous areas, and I cannot guarantee anyone's safety. We do not yet know what we are dealing with."

The pain in the old magister's eyes was obvious. His entire life had been dedicated to studying the histories of Nōl'Deron, and before him was a chance to seek out the land's original occupants. He could learn so much and write it down for future generations. No, it was too important a task to let this chance slip away.

"Your majesty, I must insist. If I die, then I die. At least let me try."

King Aelryk considered the matter sincerely. He did not like the idea of an elderly man coming along. He would not be useful if they were attacked, and he would lose a valued member of his court should tragedy befall him. The look in the old man's gray eyes spoke clearly. This would be a dream come true for him.

"Very well, Magister. I will allow you to accompany us."

"Oh, thank you, your majesty. Thank you."

"You must be ready to leave in two hours time. Do not bring any more than you need. We must travel light and with haste."

Magister Utric bowed and hurried out the door with his apprentice.

Aelryk drew his sword from its scabbard and observed it. The broad blade was etched with intricate elven runes that sparkled in the light like diamonds. Yori Half-Elven, his court blacksmith and friend, had done exquisite work on this sword. Aelryk had learned much from Yori, including tolerance. Growing up in a time when elves were an enemy had not made their friendship easy.

Nonetheless, they had become very close friends in their youth.

He re-sheathed his sword and motioned for the page to help him on with his armor. Though he would be riding through his own kingdom for a few days, he did not want to give the appearance that all was well. His subjects would see him dressed for war, and they would know he was fighting on their behalf.

With him would travel Magister Utric, Court Mage Willdor, General Morek and a company of guards. He hoped that Mi'tal's group had received his message and would be waiting for him at Duana. With any luck, he had at least one Wild Elf scout with him who could be invaluable on this journey. Perhaps Wild Elves knew more about the Westerling Elves and would be willing to share the information. If not, the scout would still be a valuable asset in avoiding the monsters of the woods.

Aelryk stepped outside in the sun and sniffed the air. Orzi was right about the day's weather. He had picked a perfect day to set out. Hopefully, his other prophecies would turn out to be correct as well.

The king headed towards the armory where Yori was busy carving runes into chamfrons for the horses. He stood with his shoulders stooped over his workbench and meticulously chiseled at the steel.

Hearing footsteps approach, he looked up and saw the king. He sat down the chisel and wiped his hands on the cloth hanging from his belt.

Aelryk smiled at the sight of his friend. He was average height with green eyes and light hair. As always, he wore a headband to hide the tips of his pointed ears.

"Good morning, Yori," Aelryk said, extending his hand.

"My lord," Yori replied, nodding and grasping the king's hand. "I'm nearly finished here. These runes will help the horses stay calm and give them courage. Without them, I can't imagine how the horses might react to the sight of those monsters."

"Thank you, my friend. I know you and your apprentices have been working very hard to complete this armor in time." Aelryk went silent for a moment. "Perhaps you could check over my sword and make sure everything is in order." He drew the sword and handed it to Yori. "Perhaps the rune etchings have worn a bit."

Yori took the sword, his brow wrinkling. Aelryk was well aware that elven runes did not wear over time. He was troubled but trying not to show it. Yori inspected the sword before taking it to the grindstone to sharpen its edge. Once he was satisfied with its sharpness, he began polishing the sword, occasionally glancing back at his friend. Silently, Aelryk watched Yori work.

"It's perfect, my king," Yori said as he handed the sword back to him.

Taking the sword, Aelryk said, "I thank you again, my friend. I also have a question for you."

Yori waited for the king to speak.

"You spent time learning from the Wild Elves and also from Enlightened Elves. Tell me, do you know anything of the Westerling Elves or of the Vale where they live? Do they even exist?"

"I wish I could help you," Yori said sincerely. "I know nothing of them. All I have heard are old fairy tales. No one has ever mentioned to me that they might actually exist."

Aelryk took a deep breath and said, "I was afraid you would say that. I wonder if I'm riding on a fool's errand." He shook his head.

"I do believe they once existed," Yori offered. "The stories say they are the First Ones. They came before all other elves, men, and dwarves. I can't see such a people going off into oblivion. I think they still exist somewhere in this world. That's truly what I believe if that helps you at all, my friend."

"It does help. I'll leave you to finish your work." Aelryk shook his friend's hand once again.

As he left the armory, his mind was still uneasy. Perhaps Yori was justified in his beliefs and perhaps not. He only wished he had more solid evidence before he set out. If this was indeed an error, he would be leaving his people unattended for nothing.

A few blocks down the stone path were the king's stables. The troops who would accompany him were already gathered and preparing their horses. His wife Lisalla and son Rykon were making their way towards him. They would want to see him off on his journey.

He walked past the stables to meet his wife. Her tall, slender form was accentuated by the dark blue gown she wore. Her blonde ringlets rested lazily on her breast. Taking both of her hands in his, he kissed her softly on each cheek.

"My queen," he said.

"My lord," she replied. "Rykon and I were just coming to wish you good journey."

"We're still waiting for Mage Willdor and Magister Utric to arrive. I have a little time if you would like to join me for a drink."

"I'd be delighted," she said, and they headed for the market area together.

Rykon, who had been distracted by a smile from a pretty young maid, followed a short distance behind. He was a handsome youth and often caught the eye of the young ladies in town. At only sixteen, he was already as tall as his father and had the same dark hair and eyes.

The three of them took a seat near the inn and called for the serving girl to bring them each some wine. The young girl hurried away and reappeared almost instantly bearing three goblets. She placed the drinks in front of the royal family and then curtsied, her ample bosom leaning in towards Rykon. The view was not lost on him, and he gave an approving smile.

"How long will you be away, father," he asked.

"A few weeks at the least," Aelryk answered. "The maps are quite old, but if they are correct, the journey to the Vale will take at least a week on horseback. Then there is the matter of crossing a river of unknown depth and width."

"But the prophecy isn't specific," Lisalla said. "You may find whatever it is you need without crossing the river."

"It's possible," Aelryk said, "but the near bank is not likely a land of spring."

"Do you think you'll find elves there?" Rykon asked, sipping at his wine.

"I don't know what we'll find there," he replied. "Perhaps if they are still around they can tell me how to bring a river back with me."

"Orzi has said that the prophecy will find a way," Lisalla said, laying her hand on top of his. "An answer will be revealed to you at the right time. I'm sure of it." She leaned in and kissed his forehead.

"Shall we head back to the stables? The others are most likely waiting for me by now." Aelryk rose and laid a few coins on the table.

The trio headed back to the stable where the rest of the party was indeed waiting for the king. The men bowed their heads as he approached.

"Is everything in order?" he asked General Morek.

"Yes, my lord," Morek replied. "Everything is prepared."

"Let's get to it then," Aelryk commanded.

He turned to his wife and kissed her lips. Then, he turned to his son and hugged him.

"Safe journey, father," Rykon said.

"Be well, husband," Lisalla said with tears in her eyes. She had seen him off on journeys before, but she was always sad to see him go.

Without a word, Aelryk mounted his horse. He raised his hand in a gesture of farewell to his family and then headed to the road with his companions following closely behind.

Chapter 12

After a hard day's ride, Mel and the others arrived at Duana. Slowly, they walked their horses to the stables and dismounted.

"Well, my ass hurts," Mel said rubbing his backside.

Thinal walked behind him and squeezed his bottom with both hands. "I'll help you with that later," she said.

"Not accustomed to riding much, Mel?" Mi'tal asked.

"I'd say that's the second time in my life I've been on a horse, or maybe it's the third. I've never ridden all day before, and I don't much care to do it again."

"I'm sure the king won't want to travel on foot," Mi'tal said, "but we may have a few days rest before he arrives. Let's see if they have any rooms for us at the inn."

The six of them headed towards the inn just as the sun was disappearing below the horizon. A warm orange hue filled the sky.

The inn was rather large and in good repair. Voices could be heard coming from the common room. Duana was a medium-sized town that did not receive too many visitors, but the inn was the center of activity for its citizens.

Mi'tal and Loren stepped inside first, followed by Mel, Thinal, and the guards. Immediately, Byord and Oli took seats among the crowd and motioned to a server to bring ale. Mi'tal led the others to the bar where a fat innkeeper was hurriedly wiping glasses.

"Good evening, innkeeper," Mi'tal said. "Do you have any rooms available this night?"

The innkeeper stopped wiping glasses and looked up. His eye fell straight to Mel and Thinal, who were dressed in animal skin clothing.

"What the hell?" he said, bewildered. His eyes darted between Mi'tal and the elves.

"Forgive me, innkeeper," Mi'tal said. "I am Councilor Mi'tal, First Advisor to King Aelryk. These are my companions, Councilor Loren, Mel, and Thinal. We are on urgent business for the king and would like rooms for the night."

The innkeeper swallowed and took one more look at the elves. "Councilor, sir, this is a thing unheard of." He leaned over the bar close to Mi'tal and whispered, "Those are savages. Why have you brought them here? Are they under arrest?"

Mi'tal waved his hand. "No, nothing like that. They are in the king's employ."

The innkeeper stood up straight, dumbstruck. "We have plenty of rooms available. Two silver per night, and that includes your meals."

"Thank you, sir," Mi'tal said. "We will take five rooms." He placed ten silver coins on the bar. The price was unreasonable, of course, but he was in no mood to argue.

"Rooms are upstairs. You can take your pick," the innkeeper said, scooping up the coins. "Oh, and make sure your wild friends behave themselves. I don't want any problems."

Mi'tal nodded and motioned the others to follow him to a nearby table.

"Let's have some dinner, shall we?" Loren said. His stomach had been rumbling for hours. He was not inclined to miss a meal and had put on some weight over the last few years. A comfortable seat on the king's council had not helped his physical fitness.

A few seconds after taking their seats, the innkeeper appeared at their table with four steaming bowls of stew and a loaf of bread.

"Drinks are on their way," he said and hurried off.

They ate hungrily while Loren grabbed at the majority of the bread.

"Hey, Mel," Oli called from the corner. "There's a man over here that says he can aim better than any elf. Why don't you come over here and show him a thing or two?"

Mel looked over at Thinal who smiled and shrugged. Never one to back down from a competition, he backed his chair away from the table and headed towards Oli. Byord raised a mug as he walked by.

"This little thing?" the challenger asked, laughing. "Place your bets, gentlemen." He finished his mug of ale, slammed it on the table, and grinned.

At the rear corridor of the inn was a throwing area. It was well positioned to avoid accidents caused by intoxicated competitors.

"I'll take fifty copper on the elf," Oli said. His remark was followed by abundant laughter. Most of the others were betting against him.

"Three knives each, closest to the bull's-eye wins," the challenger said. "I'll go first so you can see how it's done."

One at a time, he turned and threw the three knives. Each one landed in the exact center of the target. The crowd cheered, and the man raised his arms and nodded his head.

Mel retrieved the knives from the wall, and the crowd once again fell silent. Positioning all three knives in his hand at once, he gave a quick flick of his wrist. Three knives stuck deeply into the target's center.

"Yes!" Oli shouted, jumping up and spilling his ale.

The crowd was obviously stunned, and many of them sat with their mouths wide open.

"Looks like a draw," Byord offered. "They both hit the center."

"Bring out the moving target!" someone in the crowd yelled. An onlooker near the railing above loosed a target that hung from the ceiling and swung side to side.

Both Mel and his competitor threw their knives and hit the center of the target.

"Looks like we'll have to move this fight outside," the challenger said, grinning.

Most of the crowd followed as the pair walked outside. Behind the inn was an archery range.

"Bows?" Mel asked, thinking how easy it was going to be to win.

"Not against an elf," his competitor huffed. "We'll throw hatchets."

Though Mel had much less practice throwing hatchets than he had throwing knives, he was still able to hit the center three times. His competitor hit the center as well.

The crowd started to get annoyed at the lack of a winner, and one man offered up a solution. "I'll throw an apple in the air and see if you can hit it. One try each."

The rest of the crowd shouted their approval. Grabbing two apples, the man tossed one high into the air. Mel threw first. His knife sliced the apple in two halves and stuck fast in the ground. The second apple flew, and Mel's competitor tossed his knife towards it. The knife's handle bounced off the apple and fell flat in the dirt.

The crowd roared and Oli shouted, "Pay up!"

Mel's competitor was livid. His face reddened as he marched towards the man who had thrown the apples. He punched him square in the face. Quickly, a brawl ensued amongst the crowd.

Mel preferred to stay out of the mess, so he walked back into the inn and sat down next to Thinal.

"Did you win?" she asked.

"Yep," he replied, downing another mug of ale.

Chapter 13

"Father, the creature's body has been taken to the House of Medicine for inspection by the Elders," Isandra said as she approached River. She was his eldest daughter and favored her mother in looks, except she had her father's deep blue eyes. Her temperament, however, was quite different from her mother. She was a warrior who preferred armor and swords to gowns and jewelry.

"Thank you, Isandra," River said, laying a hand on her shoulder. "Shall we go and have a look at it?"

"It's a horrible, ugly thing," Isandra said, frowning. "I've never seen anything quite like it. We found it dead about three days away from our village. It was seriously wounded by the dryad but managed to flee quite a distance before succumbing to its injuries."

Together they headed for the House of Medicine. It was near mid-day and a soft rain was falling. River paused and turned his face toward the sky, allowing the tiny droplets to settle upon his face. As he took a deep breath in, fresh, sweet-smelling air filled his nostrils. Opening his sapphire eyes, he turned and smiled at his daughter. They continued on their way.

Reaching their destination, they saw a few of the Elders had already gathered outside the door. They nodded in turn, acknowledging River as he passed by.

Inside, the creature's body had been placed on a soft bed. Despite its fierce appearance, its face seemed peaceful in death. River approached silently and laid his hands upon its furry head. A blue light surrounded the lifeless body.

Isandra watched her father silently as the Elders entered the room. They observed River as he examined the creature. Any information he could glean from it would help them decide what course of action to pursue. His face was serene as he penetrated the creature's mind with his magic. Many of its secrets would be revealed to him.

"This was once a woman from the Kingdom of Na'zora," River began, speaking softly. "Some evil has bound her essence. A very dark magic has combined her with the essence of a wolf from the

Wildlands. Her every action has been controlled by sorcery. She was commanded to kidnap a dryad and return her to her master."

"Who is her master?" Elder Rellin asked.

River removed his hands from her head and looked at the Elders. "She does not know his name or location. It is a compulsion that draws her to him. Her own will is long since gone. These are only fading memories that I can read. Had she been found sooner, perhaps I could learn more."

"Will they try again?" Brandor inquired, his face concerned.

"I have no doubt of it," River replied. "She was unable to succeed in her task, and I do not believe her master would give up easily."

"I will see that patrols are increased even more," Isandra said, bowing her respect to the Elders. Promptly, she turned and left to tend to her duties.

"What should we do with the body?" Rellin asked.

"Treat it with respect," River replied. "This was not always a creature of evil. She deserves her dignity in death."

Rellin nodded. River turned to leave, followed by Brandor.

Outside, the gentle rain had ended, and the clouds gave way to a bright blue sky. Small droplets of water still lingered on the lush green foliage of the Vale. Elves walked about the village casually, going about their business.

"River, my friend," Brandor said. "Do you have any idea who could be behind this?"

"Someone evil, obviously," River said with a sigh. "But a name I cannot give you. Nor have I seen this person's face. Where he is, and who he is, I simply do not know. All I know for sure is that he has not touched the Blue River, nor have these creatures. If they are indeed on both banks, they must be coming from the south and entering the land from the sea. Whoever is controlling them does not want me to know."

"That is a most distressing thought," Brandor said, shaking his head. "Not many people know that we are still here. Then again, it could just be superstition keeping them from the river. Tales of our people have been told in many lands. I'm sure most people think we are just a myth."

"Perhaps," River said, contemplating the idea. "With malice being their only intent, they would find crossing the river impossible. If they had tried, I would have seen it."

"Since they did not try," Brandor began, "then it probably wasn't just out of superstition. Whoever it is, he must be stopped." After a few moments of silence, he asked, "Could it be Telorithan?"

"It could be, but I doubt it. His method of binding a living being's essence is quite different. I suppose he could have learned a new way that requires less power, but he lives in his tower and has everything he has ever wanted. He has no reason to do this."

"Trying to understand a mind of evil is like trying to tame the wind itself." Brandor's voice was grave as he spoke.

River clapped his hand on Brandor's back and smiled. "I could not catch it or tame it, but I could try speaking with it. Perhaps the wind holds the answers we seek."

* * * * *

Evening arrived in the Vale heralded by the soft hooting of an orange-eyed owl. The sky was clear and full of stars as Lenora sat at her dresser brushing her long, golden hair. She sat down her silver brush and slipped into a long white nightdress. A soft breeze blew in from her balcony, and she welcomed its caress on her cheek.

River approached from behind and kissed her softly on her neck. "Good evening, love," he said.

She turned, wrapping her arms around his neck. She kissed his lips, looked up at him, and smiled. Taking his hand, she led him into the bedroom. He sat at the edge of the bed while Lenora went to her dresser to retrieve the hairbrush.

Sitting cross-legged on the bed behind him, she began loosening the braids he wore accenting each side of his long brown hair. Lenora herself had braided it that morning as usual. Every evening, she would loosen the braids and brush out his hair. It was a simple routine, but one she performed lovingly.

When she had finished brushing his hair, she kissed his temple and massaged his shoulders. Then, she helped him out of his clothing and into a pale blue nightshirt.

Fiddling with the white stone ring on her finger, she asked, "What troubles you, dear?"

Taking in a deep breath and releasing it slowly, he answered, "Many things."

"Lie back and ease your mind," she said.

Lying across the bed, he placed his head in her lap and closed his eyes. She placed a hand gently on his cheek and kissed his forehead. Softly, she began to hum while running her fingers through his hair.

Smiling, River opened his eyes and said, "I love you, Lenora, more than anything."

"I love you too, my River," she responded.

She moved and placed her head upon his chest and laid her hand over his heart. He embraced her as they settled in for the night. Serenity descended throughout the room as the night crept over the Vale.

Chapter 14

"Tu'vad, my lord," the mine supervisor called as he came running towards him.

Tu'vad turned and watched the middle-aged man as he ran. They must have discovered a very large gem.

"My lord," the man said, out of breath. "Look at this."

He opened his hand and held it out for Tu'vad's inspection. Inside his palm were golden flecks. They had discovered gold in one of the gem mines. The flecks were very small, but perhaps there were a lot more to be found.

"Who else is aware of this?" Tu'vad demanded.

"Just the miner who found it, sir. I came to you straight away."

"Good," Tu'vad replied. "I'd like to keep this secret. Take a few miners and separate them from the others. Have them mine only for the gold, and store any that you find in separate carts from the gems. Do not mention this to anyone else. Is that clear?"

"Yes, my lord," he replied.

Tu'vad could not believe his luck. He could keep this discovery quiet and not have to share it with Ulda. His master was so busy with his other work that a little gold should easily go unnoticed. Besides, what use did Ulda have for gold? He had his unlimited power source of human souls. Gold was nothing to him, but it meant great wealth for Tu'vad. He had to survive in the world of men where money brings ultimate power. This discovery was an excellent bonus to accompany the lands and titles Ulda was going to give him. Once he had acquired a sizeable amount of gold, he would simply kill the miners who knew about it. No one else would ever know.

* * * * *

A row of young children sat wide-eyed and terrified in Ulda's laboratory. The spiderlings had grown and were ready for the Soulbinders to practice splicing them with the souls of the children.

"As you can see, it doesn't matter the age of your specimen when you are working with humans," Ulda proclaimed. "It only matters how frightened they are. A young specimen can power your enchantments just as effectively as an older one. Brave warriors do produce a stronger enchantment, most likely due to the fact that they are more difficult to frighten. For them, it's best to capture them, torture them, and harm the ones they love. Even if you only say you're harming them, it will suffice. That is, of course, only if you aren't able to get your hands on their actual family."

Ulda had been practicing for several days and learning new techniques quite often. The process was becoming smoother and quicker. Soon, he would begin practicing on elves, but for now he had a fairly steady supply of humans just waiting to be used.

"Are the spider creatures superior to the wolves, master?" a Soulbinder asked.

"In some ways, yes," he replied. "Spiders instill a special fear in many people. Even though a wolf is more capable of harm, humans seem to have an innate fear of the spider. That makes our work of soul binding much easier. Also, these spiders have a specially designed exoskeleton that I've created with the dust from our ruined binding gems. Fragments and tiny gems that serve no other use are now providing protection for our creations."

Ulda was beaming with pride. He was certain that this dust could also be used to create armor for his Soulbinders, his troops, and any other creatures he wished to conjure. It would provide better protection than metals or leathers. He just needed to keep working and soon the process would be perfected.

"Alright, Soulbinders," he said. "Choose a child, and let's see how you're progressing."

The Soulbinders each stood in front of a child. One child, a red-haired little girl, tried to run away. She was promptly stopped by a guard who kicked her legs from under her and dragged her back to the row of children. The other children sat frozen in terror.

"Now, bind these children and merge each with a spiderling. If you succeed, the creature will be in your command. If not, you will have to obtain another child yourself before trying again."

Beams of purple light shot from the Soulbinders onto the children. They twisted and screamed but remained locked in the Soulbinders' magic. Blinding flashes began filling the room, and within minutes, twenty-five new creatures stood awaiting their commands. All of the Soulbinders had succeeded. Their diligent practice had paid off.

At nearly five feet tall with black and yellow markings, the spider hybrids were quite a terrifying sight. With foot-long pincers and a score of eyes set atop their heads, they would inspire the necessary fear to ease the binding of hundreds of souls.

"Well done, well done!" Ulda shouted and clapped his hands. His Soulbinders were ready, and his creatures were ready. It was time to test their abilities in battle. A raid on another small village would be just the thing.

"Slave!" Ulda called. A young boy ran to his side immediately. "Take a message to General Fru. Tell him to prepare battle plans for my Soulbinders and their minions. It's time for another raid."

Chapter 15

The midday sun baked down on Duana's marketplace as Mel and Thinal casually browsed the local wares. One booth in particular caught Thinal's eye. The merchants were selling metal and glass jewelry along with various trinkets and baubles.

Browsing inside the booth, she noticed a hairpin adorned with a brightly colored glass butterfly. She picked it up and twirled it with her fingers. She smiled shyly at Mel.

"That's very pretty," he said.

"It is," she replied.

"And it would look lovely on you," he added.

Mel did not carry many of the coins used for trade in Na'zora. Occasionally, he would trade wares for a small amount of them, but they were virtually worthless among the Wild Elves. Today, however, he did have a few of them on his person.

"How much?" Thinal asked, holding the pin up towards the merchant.

"Ten coppers," he replied, "but for someone as lovely as yourself, I'll make it five."

Mel fiddled in the small bag he wore on his belt and counted out five coppers. Handing them to the merchant, he said, "Thank you."

"Thank you, young sir," he replied pocketing the coins.

Thinal quickly removed the small leather strap that was holding back her ponytail and began twisting her hair up and tucking in the ends. She stuffed the pin into her twisted hair and turned her head side to side so that Mel might observe how the glass caught the light.

"You look lovely," he said, kissing her cheek.

"Thank you, Mel."

Thinal took his arm, and they continued through the marketplace. They passed a booth full of fine silks which an elf could scarcely hope to afford. Thinal brushed a hand lightly over a pale orange fabric and commented on its softness.

As they walked, they became aware that some of Duana's citizens were observing them curiously. Very few Wild Elves ever visited this far north in Na'zora. More southern villages such as Enald were used to the elven presence, but here they were something of a curiosity. The children seemed the most interested and did not turn their heads when the two elves looked in their direction. For the most part, the adults were polite, although they seemed a little distrusting. That was to be expected, however, as elves were not generally quick to trust humans either.

One bold little boy finally found the courage to approach them. "Are you elves?" he asked.

"Yes, we are," Thinal replied, smiling.

"Is that why your ears are pointy?"

"Yes, just as yours are round because you're human."

"Why is he so short?" the child asked, pointing at Mel.

"Because I didn't eat all my vegetables," Mel barked.

"My Daddy says it's eating meat that will make me tall," the little boy replied matter-of-factly, his hands on his hips.

"Mel is only teasing you," Thinal said, laughing. "Among our kind, men are generally a bit shorter than the ladies. It makes it easier to hunt and hide in the thick forests. They're also the best archers in all of Nōl'Deron."

"I've heard about that," the boy said eagerly. "I've heard the girls are good with swords too!"

"You're right we are. We carry long, broad swords that require both hands to use."

The child's eyes went wide with amazement as Thinal drew her blade and knelt down for the child to observe it. The shining blade was etched with runes that resembled leaves on a vine. He touched his hand to the green and black stones that decorated the hilt.

All of a sudden, a terrified scream pierced the air. It was quickly followed by more screaming and people running towards the market.

"Run! Hide!" Thinal yelled to the boy, who promptly took her advice.

Mel drew his bow, and together they ran towards the source of the screaming. The city guard was only a few hundred feet behind them, their weapons drawn. Terrified townspeople were fleeing through the city. Something was coming from the Wildlands.

Mel quickly climbed to the top of a nearby house to have a better look over the crowd. Thinal, sword ready, waited at the bottom. In the distance, Mel could see what had sent the townspeople fleeing. Four huge spiders, nearly as tall as he was, were making their way toward Duana. Behind them, two figures sitting atop wildcats pointed their fingers and shouted orders at the spiders.

"Giant spiders!" he yelled down to Thinal.

"What?" she asked dumbfounded.

Without replying, Mel began firing arrows as soon as the spiders were in range. Thinal ran to join the city guard in their fight against the creatures. Two guards had already been taken down by webs, and beams of purple light were extending from their struggling forms to the hooded figures riding the wildcats.

These were sorcerers, Thinal realized. Instead of fighting wolfish monsters as she had expected, she was now fighting giant spiders. Things were definitely getting more and more strange in the world of men.

Avoiding the purple beams, Thinal ran towards one of the spiders. It saw her coming and tossed a web. She dodged, pirouetting to her right, and was quickly confronted by a second spider. Bringing her sword down in one quick motion, she removed a leg from the spider. Pus began spewing from the wound, and she coughed as the stench reached her nostrils.

Without missing a step, she swung behind the stunned creature and brought down another blow on its back. It fell to the ground under the weight of her sword. Quickly, she positioned herself beside it and sliced its head from its body. This time the stench was nearly overwhelming, but she managed to compose herself and carry on.

She turned to find the spider who had tossed a web at her lying dead just a few paces away with an arrow sticking out of its head. While one sorcerer was busy extending a beam towards a third downed soldier, Thinal took the opportunity to move in closer. She crept towards him, using the trees as cover. All of a sudden, the wildcat noticed her and roared. The sorcerer's concentration broke just as she hurled herself from behind a tree and swung hard with her sword. With a thud, the sorcerer landed hard on the ground, clutching at his nearly-severed thigh. She finished him off quickly, before he could cast any more spells.

An arrow landed in the wildcat's neck and it reared wildly as blood poured from the artery that had been hit. With its last strength, it charged toward her, but a second arrow hit the back of its head and stopped it permanently.

She caught sight of the second sorcerer, who had apparently realized he couldn't handle enemies that would fight back. He turned his wildcat and headed back off into the forest, followed by the remaining two spiders. In all, five of the city guard had been taken down and been subjected to the purple light beam of the sorcerers.

Mel ran to Thinal. "Are you hurt?" he asked, breathing heavily.

"I'm just a little dirty," she replied.

"Should we go after them?" he asked.

"I think we should go find Mi'tal. He's going to want to see these creatures and the sorcerer too. Maybe he's learned more about what's actually going on here."

A crowd had begun to gather around the site of the attack. Seeing the last of the monsters flee, they had decided to come and have a better look. Pushing through the crowd was Mi'tal, followed closely by Loren.

"Are you two alright?" he asked hastily.

"We're fine," Mel said. "What in hell are these things?"

"I have no idea," he replied. "I've never heard of such a thing, and there have been no previous attacks on Duana."

Loren knelt next to a fallen city guard. He brushed away the webbing and turned the man onto his back. His face was twisted into an expression of terror and pain. Whispering a prayer, Loren brushed his hand over the man's face to close his eyes. Next, he observed the carcass of the slain spider. He looked back at Mi'tal, tears in his eyes.

"I have never seen such horror," he said, wiping away a tear.

"Come, all of you," Mi'tal said. "I'll have the bodies brought into the city, and we can have a better look there."

The surviving members of the city guard carried away their fallen comrades. Duana's apothecary and his apprentices came to claim the bodies of the spiders, wildcat, and sorcerer. They would be taken to his establishment where the local doctors and mages would be able to study them.

"I need to change into some clean clothes before I do anything else," Thinal declared. "I smell terrible, and I can't imagine how disgusting I must look."

"We'll stop at the inn," Mel said.

"Meet us at the city hall as quickly as you can, then," Mi'tal said. "I'm sure the mayor will have many questions about what you saw. He will also want to thank you."

Mel nodded and set off toward the inn with Thinal. Another crowd was forming along the road past the inn. Horsemen with banners were arriving as the crowd began to cheer. King Aelryk had arrived in Duana.

Chapter 16

Morning in the Vale brought a beautiful sunny day. The weather was mild, the birds were singing, and the smell of flowers filled the air. Lenora waited patiently on the bank for her life mate to finish his ritual. A yellow butterfly floated lazily and landed upon her shoulder. She smiled at it and turned her gaze back to River, who was emerging from the water.

Helping him don his robe, she said, "I need to gather some healing herbs. Would you walk with me?"

"I'd be delighted," he said, and he kissed her cheek.

She grabbed her basket from the silver bench nearby and slipped her arm in his. The two walked slowly along the bank of the river.

"Perhaps we should speak with the dryads. They may have helpful information for us," he suggested.

"I'd enjoy that. I haven't visited with the ladies in some time now."

Smiling, she turned her face toward the sun. She enjoyed the warmth for a few seconds and then laid her head on River's shoulder. He kissed the top of her golden head, and they continued on along the bank.

She stopped at a small bunch of heart-shaped leaves growing on a vine. Clipping two leaves, she placed them inside her basket. A fallen log offered a few brown mushrooms that would serve nicely as medicines. Ahead of them in the forest, they spotted Rogin on his patrol.

"Good morning, Mother, Father," he said, waving to them.

Lenora hugged him and kissed his cheek. "Good morning, son," she said. "How is everything today?"

"We haven't noticed anything unusual. Are you heading out into the forest?"

"We are going to visit with the dryads," River responded.

"I haven't spotted a single dryad since we found the one injured. Please don't travel too far."

"We'll be safe," Lenora said, brushing Rogin's dark hair away from his eyes.

River knelt to the ground and placed a hand on the soft earth. Closing his eyes, he sensed the water deep beneath them. Following it, he detected the deepest roots of the trees in a nearby area of forest. Dryads are creatures of the trees, and their roots run deep as well. He could feel their presence as well as the source of water they were using to sustain themselves.

"I have located them," he said, returning to his feet. "They've moved a little more south, but it isn't very far."

"I will bid you good journey, then," Rogin said.

They continued on their way, stopping occasionally for Lenora to gather leaves and flowers. Her basket was nearly half full, and she was quite pleased at the abundance of the herbs she needed. She glanced over to her left and saw an almond tree in full bloom. Smiling at her life mate she proceeded toward the tree. Almonds were his very favorite food, so she picked a handful and placed them in her basket.

"That's very thoughtful of you," he said.

A few miles through the forest, the trees became more dense. River stopped and raised a hand in the air, listening. Opening his eyes, he peeked around a tree to the right. He caught a glimpse of a dryad observing the two of them.

"Greetings, sisters," he said. "We've come to speak with you."

Four dryads emerged from their trees and approached them. They were each tall and slender with bright green eyes. Three had silvery skin, while one was tawny. Their hair matched their skin, with strands of leaves woven throughout it.

"Greetings, River and Lenora," the tawny dryad spoke. "We are pleased that you have come here."

"We are so sorry about the loss of one of your sisters. It was an unspeakable evil," Lenora said.

"Your condolences are appreciated," the dryad replied. "It was a great loss."

"Did you witness the attack?" asked River.

"I did not, sadly. I wish with all my heart I could have been of assistance. None of us here saw what happened, but we felt it."

"We found the body of the creature responsible," River said. "It was a hybrid created using a human and a wolf. Someone had bound their essences and ordered them to kidnap a dryad."

"I pray to the Earth that the person responsible is stopped. Free creatures live on in agony once their souls are bound."

A loud growl thundered through the air, startling them all.

"Behind me, ladies," River commanded.

Lenora and the dryads obeyed, moving close behind River. The roar sounded again, this time followed by footsteps. Three of the wolf creatures were running towards them.

Extending his right arm, his palm facing outward, River created a shield wall of water between them and the creatures. They ran into his shield, attacking it wildly. Despite their best efforts, they could not penetrate it.

With his left hand, River sent a blast of blue energy into one of them, knocking it unconscious. He did the same with the other two. When all three lay unconscious, he lowered the shield.

"Can you release them from this spell?" a silvery dryad asked.

"I can try," he said, placing a hand on one creature's forehead. He leaned in close, placing his ear near the creature's face. He listened as the essence trapped within began to tell him its tale.

"Once this creature was a young man from a village called Enald in Na'zora," River began. "He remembers his village being attacked, and he tried to help the women and children escape. He grabbed a hay fork and charged at the attackers. They were sorcerers. He remembers a flash of light and then waking up in this form. He was taken far south and placed on a ship. After a few days, he was released with three others upon this coast and commanded to bring back dryads, nymphs, and any other creature of magical design. He does not know the name or location of his true master. He begs for the release of death."

"Is there any way to save them?" Lenora asked, kneeling next to the pitiable creature.

"Both man and wolf are already dead. I cannot release their souls on my own. The enchantment is far too strong. Joining powers with a second elemental could help, but I do not sense any nearby."

"Fire lives in a tower only a few days from here," offered one of the dryads.

"He will not help. I know him far too well to ask. None of my more benevolent brothers are near enough. Our only chance is to give them to the river. There, they may find peace with the Spirit of the water."

Three more dryads appeared from their trees and helped carry the sleeping bodies to the bank of the Blue River. Slowly, they placed them on the surface and watched as they sank and disappeared. A gentle rain began to fall as the Earth mourned. The evil that had corrupted the creatures held no more sway. The river had freed them, and the wind carried in it a sense of relief.

"We should head back," Lenora said.

"A gift, Lenora, before you go," a russet-colored dryad said. "Take this bark for brewing as tea. It is difficult to find and has excellent medicinal qualities."

Lenora accepted the gift and thanked the dryad. With all four creatures accounted for, the dryads would be safe for now. They said their goodbyes as the dryads returned to their trees.

Together, River and Lenora walked along the river bank back toward the Vale. The sun was setting, and the sky was filled with orange and pink. A few birds still sang, hoping to get in one more song before nightfall. Fireflies blinked in the distance.

As they arrived home, Alyra waved and called out to greet them. She ran to River, who picked her up and hugged her.

"It's bedtime for you, little one," he said.

"I know, but I was waiting for you."

"Outside in your nightdress," Lenora added.

River carried her inside and tucked her into her bed. Once she was settled he sat at the edge of her bed and sang softly to her.

The sun has gone down, and the birds cease to peep.
Let the sound of the water drift you to sleep.

The stars shine brightly, and the moon sends her beams.
It's time to enter the world of dreams.

I'll keep you safe throughout the night
and wake you again at morning's first light.

Alyra yawned and drifted off to sleep. River kissed her forehead and took Lenora's hand. Outside under the stars, he held his love tightly in his arms. A cool breeze blew in and rustled the leaves as frogs sang softly to the night.

Chapter 17

"Fool! Idiot!" Ulda shouted as he slapped the cowering Soulbinder across his face.

"Mercy, master!" the elf cried.

"Mercy? For you? You were supposed to await orders! You were never supposed to command your own attack! You may have wanted to gain glory, but all you've brought is ruin! Four ruined souls you've given me, not to mention the loss of two spiders, a wildcat, and a very promising Soulbinder!"

Ulda was far beyond angry. Not only had this attack been a waste of lives, it had given the humans the impression that they were easily defeated.

"Wild Elves, no less, alongside a handful of useless human guards! Not a sorcerer among them, yet you were driven back with heavy losses!"

"Please, master," the elf pleaded. "Let me make this up to you, please!"

"Oh you will. Restrain him!" he commanded the other Soulbinders.

Immediately, they all unleashed their magic upon the cowering form. He was held frozen in place, his face twisting in agony.

Ulda placed a gem into his glowing orb and unleashed a bolt of lightning on his former Soulbinder. The elf screamed in pain and contorted his body despite being held in place by the other sorcerers. His cries lasted several minutes as Ulda had planned. He did not intend for this one to die in peace. He would serve as an example to the others. Any disobedience would be met with severe punishment.

Finally, the lifeless elf slumped to the ground. Ulda removed the gem from the orb and handed it to one of the Soulbinders.

"Take this to the master jeweler," he ordered. "I want this gem set into a necklace. I will add this one's power to my own." He kicked the former Soulbinder's corpse as he spoke. "Get rid of that," he said casually.

The others rushed to fulfill his commands. No one else wanted to risk facing his anger.

Storming into the throne room, Ulda sat down hard upon his chair. Tu'vad, who had been waiting within, bowed low.

"What news?" Ulda asked sharply.

"Your majesty, gems have been sent up by the cartload. At your request, the smallest have been ground into dust. We still have not located any very large stones, but the miners are working very hard under my supervision."

"Very good," Ulda said, sounding bored. "I need to strengthen the defenses of our hybrid creatures. Apparently the runed swords and bows of the Wild Elves have been able to penetrate the spiders' exoskeletons. Normal human weapons have proven just as useless as before."

"Perhaps steel armor could be runed, and your sorcerers could combine the strength of souls to the dust."

"Dust cannot hold an essence, and spiders cannot move freely in steel armor. Your idea may benefit our troops, however. Perhaps the dust could be enchanted through the same process and be incorporated into the runes. That just might work!" Ulda's eyes became wide with excitement. "As far as the spiders, though, we need something else. A new process for grafting the dust into their exoskeletons must be found." Ulda hopped from his throne with a newfound vigor. "I'll be in my laboratory. See that I'm not disturbed!"

* * * * *

Hours passed and Ulda still stood bent over his table staring into his orb. He was pondering the idea that dust could indeed hold a soul. These dark gems were very strong, however, they still had to be cut properly in order to contain the essence. If they were fractured, they were useless. He had already tried restoring broken gems, but he had no success.

Before turning his immense talents to mysticism, Ulda had been a master of potion-making at a very young age. Perhaps returning to his roots held the answer. Quickly, he grabbed a phial from a nearby shelf and placed a handful of gem dust inside. His alchemy equipment was rarely used, but it was of a very high quality. He moved over to the cabinets and began grabbing at different ingredients. A smile crept across his face as he realized this could actually work.

After combining a number of ingredients and setting them to cook over a flame, he started to become anxious. He chewed at his lip impatiently, waiting for the concoction to finish brewing. Once it had changed to a pale peach color, it was ready. Now, he needed to test it on something.

"Slave!" he called, turning his head towards the door.

A young boy peeked inside the lab.

"Have a spiderling sent up immediately," he commanded.

Setting the potion aside to cool, he began to pace across the room. If the young spider could ingest the concoction without dying, it would be a good start. Testing on a fully grown spider was too much of a risk. He had already lost two and didn't want to lose another without very good cause.

After a few moments, the slave boy reappeared with a spiderling in a jar. Ulda snatched the creature away.

"Stay put, slave," he ordered.

He drew a small amount of the potion into a dropper and fed it to the tiny spider. It was still for only a second before a glow spread over its entire body. It gave one shiver followed by a high pitched squeak, and then it stood perfectly still.

Ulda could tell it was still alive, but the results seemed a little disappointing. All of a sudden, the spider's exoskeleton took on a shine. Excited that his potion was working, he opened the jar and spilled the spider onto the ground. The slave boy jumped back, his eyes wide. Ulda stomped on the spider as it fell to the floor. Moving his foot to see under it, he realized that the spider was still very much alive.

"Wonderful!" Ulda shouted.

He picked the spider up from the floor and examined it. It appeared to be completely undamaged. His potion had truly worked. Perhaps it would work for his wolf hybrids as well. It might work for his troops, but their souls would need to be bound first. He couldn't risk an indestructible elf or human running around that was not fully under his control. Perhaps he would need to hybridize his entire army.

Chapter 18

King Aelryk had perched himself on the mayor's seat in Duana's city hall. It was a surprisingly large wooden building with quite an elaborate meeting room. The beams and supports were all decorated with scrolling patterns carved into their surfaces and several fancy brass candelabras fed light into the room.

"Your majesty, I present our elven comrades Mel and Thinal of the Silver Birch Clan," Mi'tal said gesturing toward the two elves.

They stood motionless, awaiting the king to commence speaking. They would not bow as humans do. He was not their king, and they did not plan to bow before anyone.

Aelryk observed the pair and judged Thinal to be quite lovely. She had a friendly nature about her, unlike her companion. He appeared standoffish and distrustful.

"I hear you two put up quite the fight against the invaders. You have my thanks for saving the lives of my citizens."

Mel stood stone-faced as he did not care to hear this king's appreciation. He was no hero, and he had not set out to save human lives. He was preserving his own life and that of his mate and nothing more.

"We're glad to be of assistance, your majesty," Thinal said politely.

Aelryk glanced at Mi'tal who stood silently next to Mel. "Mi'tal has told me that you have some news of a situation in Al'marr?"

After a few seconds of silence, Thinal nudged Mel with her elbow.

"Yes, I do," Mel began reluctantly. "They have not allowed us elves to enter their markets for the last few months. The last time I was there, few villagers were still in the area. I heard rumors that the royal family had been murdered, and a sorcerer from Ral'nassa had seized the throne."

"You didn't mention that to us before," Mi'tal said, a little surprised.

"You didn't ask," Mel replied casually.

"That is grave news indeed," Aelryk said. "Do you have any knowledge of who this sorcerer might be?"

"I never heard his name. All I heard was that he had some inside help to take the throne, and the people were frightened. I have seen the wolfbeasts returning through the Wildlands to the borders of Al'marr. Today is the first I've seen of the spiders."

"What of the sorcerers? Is this the first you've seen of them?" Aelryk leaned in while asking the question.

"Yes. The creatures I saw were only accompanied by the Na'zorans they had taken."

"Your people did not try to stop them?" the king asked.

Mel sighed, "No, we didn't. It wasn't our fight. We might lose half our clan to save a few of your people. Who would be left to protect our children when the monsters started coming for us?"

A brief silence followed.

"You do make a good point, Mel," the king replied. "In wartime, we must do what we can to protect our own. Sometimes it involves making difficult decisions. I am grateful you have come and have given me this information. Perhaps there should be more communication between our two peoples."

"That shouldn't be difficult seeing as you own all of the land surrounding our forests. Send someone to shout toward the trees from time to time and see if anyone responds."

Aelryk decided it was best to ignore the comment. Relations between Na'zora and the Wild Elves were still very much strained, and he knew the matter deserved his attention. A more pressing matter, however, was brewing far south in Al'marr. His people were being murdered and others taken prisoner for some unknown purpose. Until his citizens were safe again, he would not bother with any other matters of state.

"Shall we go and have a look at these beasts?" Aelryk asked as he rose from his seat.

"I think we've seen them close enough, your majesty," Thinal answered respectfully.

"Then we will speak again very soon." He nodded at the elves. "Mi'tal, Willdor, and Morek with me." The three men headed for the door.

"Highness," Magister Utric called. "For posterity, I would like to see them as well. I would like to describe them in our chronicles."

"Come along," the king replied.

Mel and Thinal waited until the men had left to make their own exit. Outside, the townspeople were busy cleaning up. The crowds running away from the attackers had done quite a bit of damage to the marketplace.

A young girl in a pink smock was struggling with a heavy barrel. Mel ignored her, but Thinal cleared her throat and inclined her head towards the girl. Sighing, Mel walked over, grabbed the barrel, and set it upright.

"Thank you, milord," the girl said with a curtsey.

Mel laughed and said, "Lord?" He looked at the girl and shook his head.

"Forgive me," she replied. "Are you a prince?"

Thinal couldn't help but laugh a little at the question. Mel grinned and continued to shake his head.

"We have no lords or princes, sweet child," Thinal said. "We are just ordinary people like yourself. We're all equals. No princes, and no lords or ladies."

"But I saw you fight. Surely you are highborn knights!"

"Your people call us Wild Elves," Mel said. "We are elves of the woodlands, and we all learn to fight this way. It keeps us safe in a dangerous world. You could learn to fight as well."

"Girls aren't allowed," she said, looking at the ground.

"Women are just as capable in battle as men. We may play different roles, but you can see that my blade is no different from the ones your men wield." Thinal drew the blade and handed it to the girl. She reached out with one skinny arm and took the sword by its hilt.

"I can barely lift this," she said. "It's very pretty, but I could never be a swordswoman." She extended the blade back to Thinal, who took it and placed it back in her scabbard.

"You could some day. You just need to work on your strength. Don't ever let anyone say you can't do something just because you're a girl. When they say that, you punch them right in the nose." Thinal punched a fist into the palm of her other hand and nodded. The young girl laughed and nodded back.

"A knee in the crotch works well too," Mel added, winking. Turning to Thinal he asked, "What do we do now?"

"Let's get something to drink," she said. "A large something."

"Fine with me as long as it's also something strong," he replied.

* * * * *

Aelryk knelt and leaned closely towards the deceased spider. The apothecary had laid it on a bed of straw in the store room of his shop. A pale greenish pus still oozed from its severed leg and head. He dipped a finger in the substance, smelled it, and immediately shuddered.

"I have collected samples of the pus, but I haven't yet had the time to test it," the white-haired apothecary said. "It smells quite foul, and it could possibly be toxic." He handed a small towel to the king, who graciously accepted it.

Duana's physician stood near the body of the fallen sorcerer. "I have examined the body of the sorcerer, your majesty, and have determined nothing significant. He is a member of the Enlightened Elf race and probably rather young by their standards, but I don't see anything unusual about him. The wildcat appears to be quite ordinary as well. It is very surprising he was able to tame it, but these magicians can work their illusions on people and beasts alike."

Court Mage Willdor rolled his eyes. Most physicians did not have respect for mages. They believed magic consisted of tricks and devilry and offered no real solutions. "If everything here is so ordinary," he began, "why did they bother to attack this city?"

"They're madmen!" the physician replied heatedly. "They summoned these evil creatures with one of their illusions."

"What do you make of the purple beams reported by the witnesses?" Willdor asked.

"They used some sort of magical energy attack. I examined the bodies of the guards, and apart from spider bites, they have no marks on them. These are vicious magical elves intent on murder for their own pleasure."

"It was elves who saved this town," Mi'tal injected, to the dismay of the physician.

"Willdor, what do you make of the purple light?" Aelryk asked. "Was it an attack? Witnesses said the guards were already down when the spell was cast."

"I can't be certain, majesty. Had it been an attack, it would have left a mark on the skin. The color of the magic would suggest they were absorbing something."

"They probably absorbed their energies to power more dark magic," the physician spat.

"Thank you, physician," the king said. "Thank you as well, apothecary. Mi'tal, I'd like to head out in the morning if at all possible. I think it would be best to send Loren back to the palace. He can inform our generals of the new threat."

"And he isn't much fun as a traveling companion anyway," Mi'tal added with a grin.

"There is that as well," the king agreed.

Chapter 19

Dawn fell over Duana, bringing with it a pink summer sky. The air was already hot and thick. Roosters were crowing while merchants once again began reopening their shops. The previous day's events were all but forgotten as the citizens strove to go about their daily lives.

Mel and Thinal headed out of the inn to meet up with their group. Thinal wished there was time for another glass of tea, but Mi'tal had been adamant when he informed them to be ready to leave at dawn. She wondered how many days it would take before they reached the Vale.

Arriving at the meeting point at the edge of the woods, they were spied by Mi'tal. "Good morning," he said cheerfully.

"Ah," said Aelryk, peeking around his horse. "Good morning. I'd like a word with you both before we set out."

Mel ignored him, went over to his horse, and began placing items into a saddlebag.

"He's not much of a morning person," Thinal said apologetically.

"I can tell he's quite obstinate," Aelryk replied. "I hope that won't pose a problem in our travels. We do need his help."

"Yes, you do. I'm no tracker, and it doesn't appear you've brought any other archers with you."

"Tell me, my lady. What do you know about the Vale?"

"Just what I've heard in fairy tales, majesty," she giggled a little. "I never even dreamed the place actually existed. The legends say it is home to Mistonwey, one of the gods our people worshipped in ancient times. We still revere all of nature, of course, but we don't actually believe the old gods exist. I wouldn't mind meeting one, though, if it's actually there."

"I don't think we're going to be finding any gods," he replied. "As a matter of fact, I'm going to find a river."

"Well, the Blue River is the largest, and the Vale supposedly lies on the distant bank. How do you plan to cross it?"

"I'm not entirely sure."

"It's always nice to travel prepared," Mel interjected as he moved to stand next to Thinal.

"You're our guide, Mel," Thinal said. "How do we cross the river?"

"Build a raft," he replied.

"Problem solved then," Aelryk said.

Mel looked at the king and asked, "Are *all* of these people coming with us? We need to move light."

"I think you should take a small army with you, your majesty," Loren offered.

"A big group is going to stand out and make an easy target. We should try not to draw attention to ourselves," Mi'tal chimed in.

"I'm inclined to agree," Aelryk responded.

"Good," Mel said. "Now we just have the thunder of steel boots and horses galloping to ruin any chance at stealth."

"We cannot walk there, master elf," Aelryk said. "It is a seven day journey on horseback, and I will not bear any delays."

"Majesty, I can offer some assistance in covering our noise and tracks," Court Mage Willdor said. "I am bringing a good supply of potions to provide you with ample magical assistance."

"Let's hope that's enough, then," Mi'tal replied. "Who will be travelling with us, your majesty?"

"Loren, you will head back to the palace with two guards of your choosing. The rest of my guards will remain here in Duana to provide protection to my people. Mi'tal, Willdor, Morek, and Utric are with me."

"My apprentice-," Utric began.

"Is too young and unable to fight for himself," Aelryk finished. "You are also unable to fight, and we do not need more people to look after. Send him back to the palace with your information on the spiders."

"Yes, my lord," he replied without arguing.

"Mel, do you know how to find the Vale?" Mi'tal asked.

"I think it's at the end of a rainbow or something," he replied sarcastically. "I can get you to the place where it supposedly exists."

"Good," Aelryk replied. "Let's get moving."

The men said their goodbyes to those who were heading back to the palace. Byord grinned and waved goodbye to Mel as he mounted his horse. He blew a kiss at Thinal, who rolled her eyes and shook her head.

The seven of them set out west in search of the Vale. Upon entering the woods, Mel pointed out the tracks left by the fleeing sorcerer and spiders. They headed off south, just as he expected. The forest was unusually quiet, and they pressed on as quickly and quietly as possible.

Chapter 20

Tu'vad headed up the twisted dirt path leading through the gray rock. All of the commotion he was hearing had better be for a good reason, otherwise the mine supervisor would answer to him for not quelling the disturbance. Nearing the mine entrance, he saw a group of miners all huddled around a small table. The supervisor caught his eye and waved.

"Lord Tu'vad! You must come and see!" he shouted.

Tu'vad continued his approach as the miners cleared the way for him to see the prize laying on the table. A deep purple gem, as large as his head, lay before him. His eyes widened, and his jaw dropped slightly in disbelief. All the times he had reassured Master Ulda that they were searching diligently for larger stones had just been a farce. Of course they were working hard, but he hadn't truly believed gems this size existed. Ulda was going to be very pleased with him indeed.

"This must be brought to Master Ulda at once," Tu'vad said.

"Right away, sir," one of the miners responded.

"Not you," Tu'vad said, noticing a young woman emerging from the mine. "You there," he shouted to her. "Grab a cart and load this gem inside it."

The young woman nodded and obeyed quickly.

"Follow me," he ordered, and the two of them set off down the path. It was only a fifteen minute walk to the palace entrance, but the heat of the summer sun was intense. Tu'vad observed the woman as sweat beads rolled down her neck and dampened her hair. She was quite lovely, despite being rather dirty.

Together they entered the palace and proceeded to Ulda's laboratory. A young slave boy stood watch outside the door.

"His majesty has commanded that he not be disturbed," the boy said.

Ulda stopped in his tracks and slapped the boy across his face. "You don't give me orders, slave. Get out of my way!" He shoved the boy away, knocking him to the ground. Flinging open the doors he shouted, "Your Highness, I've come on most urgent business."

The laboratory was in disarray and smelled of burning metals. The room was dark except for the light emitting from the orb within. All was silent, and there was no sign of movement.

Tu'vad spoke again. "Forgive my intrusion, sire, but I have brought with me that which you are seeking. It's a gemstone, majesty. It's the largest one I've seen." He heard what sounded like an iron bar being dropped to the floor. The orb's light faded, and with a snap of his fingers, Ulda flooded the room with a soft white light.

"Bring it to me," he said.

Tu'vad grabbed the cart from the woman and waved her away. He pushed it inside the lab and smiled triumphantly.

Ulda gaped at the enormous gem. This was indeed a great find. With the proper shape, this would suit his purpose perfectly. "Take it to my master jeweler. I will follow shortly with the exact details of the cut I need." As he spoke, he fiddled with the gemstone necklace he wore. Tu'vad noticed what appeared to be a face embedded within the gem. It swirled within a white mist, and he could just make out the features of the Soulbinder who had disappointed Ulda a few days earlier.

"I will take it to him personally, sire," Tu'vad said. He bowed and pushed the cart out of the lab.

Ulda began rummaging through a stack of books laying on the floor near his enchanting area. Grabbing a red volume in his hands, he flipped quickly through its pages. Arriving at the correct page, his eyes read the instructions hungrily. It would have to be oval-shaped and contain hundreds of facets. The gem was sufficiently large, and he did not doubt he would have the power to use it. With this stone and the extra power he gained from his former Soulbinder, he should be able to control all of his troops. They would fight without question and be incapable of fear.

Energized, Ulda ran out of his laboratory clutching the red book in his hand. He ran down the stone corridor and burst through the door to the jeweler's workshop. The old man looked stunned as he saw Ulda appear.

"Your majesty," he said, bowing. He was shocked but not so much that he forgot his manners.

Ulda slammed the book down on the jeweler's table and opened it to the page specifying the precise details needed for the gem. "Follow these instructions to the letter. I cannot afford to have this gem destroyed."

Ulda turned to leave as the old man began poring over the book. This was meticulous work that would take some time to complete. He had no doubt he could do what the sorcerer commanded, but he feared what purpose it might serve. However, he was in no place to question him. That would only lead to his death, and someone else would step up to serve instead. He sat at his bench and began the tedious work.

Chapter 21

Three uneventful days had passed as the companions headed for the Western Vale. The morning of the fourth day was heralded by the birds singing high in the trees. They chipped and sang and played on the wind without a care for the troubles of men.

Long days of riding were beginning to wear on the group. King Aelryk had insisted on haste, which left little time to rest or stretch the tight muscles that were forced into the same position for hours at a time. The horses were much more comfortable than their riders.

The summer heat did not help matters as it lay heavily in the dense forest. The humid air was filled with the scent of leaves and bark as if the trees themselves were sweating.

Mel led on throughout the morning as the others followed silently. The night had not spared them from the heat, and they were all still a bit tired. Finally, the trees gave way and a clearing lay in front of them. The sparse trees gave way to brilliant sunbeams, lighting the path to a meadow of purple flowers.

Mel dismounted to have a closer look at the ground. He was uneasy leading the group out into the open without first being sure it was safe. Seeing no signs of any disturbance, he signaled the others to wait while he scouted ahead. Once he had surveyed the area, he remounted and motioned for the others to follow.

Despite the lack of shade, the meadow was cooler than the forest. A cool breeze was swirling all around them as the wildflowers danced in delight. An open field lay ahead in the distance.

Mel turned his horse to speak with the king. "There is open field ahead. That means no cover should there be anything looking for us."

"What are the alternatives?" he replied.

"We could detour north. The Oak Leaf Clan has a settlement about a day's ride from here."

"I fear we would lose too much time. Let's cross here as quickly as possible."

They set out across the field of endless golden stalks. What had appeared to be small enough to cross quickly turned out to be deceptively large. This crossing was going to take over an hour at a good pace. Far in the distance, another forest beckoned to them.

Mel felt as if he had held his breath throughout the crossing. Once the forest's edge was in sight, he felt safe enough to take a deep breath. Here under the cover of trees, he was at home. He halted immediately upon entering the forest. It was quiet here-too quiet. No sound of bird nor scurrying of foraging creatures could be heard. The grass was still and his horse neighed nervously.

Suddenly, a blast of energy surged toward them, knocking them all from their mounts. The horses reared and bolted through the forest in a panic. Mel drew his bow as the others drew their weapons. He knocked an arrow and released it at the oncoming noise of running footsteps. An inhuman yowl went up as the arrow found a target. "Wolf monsters! " he cried as one stepped into view. The sorcerer, still unseen, let loose another blast of energy that scattered the travelers in all directions.

Quickly, they scrambled back to their feet and readied their weapons, spreading apart for their own safety. Staying close to each other for this fight would only make them easier targets for the sorcerer.

Thinal moved towards Utric, who was unarmed. "Stay down, and I'll protect you!" she shouted as the enemy advanced. The terrified old man obeyed.

Mel loosed another arrow, finishing off the wounded beast who had moved into view. A flash of light sped his way as he rolled sideways, narrowly avoiding it. Blindly, he fired another arrow at the source of the light, hoping it might find its mark. Willdor crouched low to the ground and released an energy blast of his own. Yelps arose from the monsters as they had not expected the hit.

"Now!" Aelryk cried to his men as the three of them rushed the stunned creatures. Thinal followed closely behind, leaving Utric well hidden in the tall grass.

Mel raced up a tall tree nearby to get a better view of the sorcerer. Reaching a wide branch, he crept out onto it and caught sight of the elf. He was mounted atop a wildcat and protected by four giant spiders. More wolfbeasts were closing in as well. There were at least a dozen of them, to Mel's count.

Once the new wave of wolfbeasts had moved into his view, Willdor unleashed another blast. His power was draining quickly, and his potions had been carried away by his frightened horse. Human mages do not naturally regenerate their magical powers as elves do. In a matter of moments, he would be completely useless in this fight.

Mel loosed arrows at the spiders, hoping to take out a few before they reached his companions. As his arrow hit one spider between its head and neck, Mel was stunned to see it glance off without injuring the beast. Unwilling to waste another shot, he aimed for the tiny eyes on the top of its head. At this distance it looked like a speck of dust, but it was his only hope. He held his breath as the arrow flew through the air. In a matter of seconds, the arrow landed, piercing straight through the eye of the beast. It flopped over immediately, its legs curling inward as it fell.

The enraged sorcerer began blasting fireballs in Mel's direction. Luckily, he was hidden by leaves and took the opportunity to take down a second spider. Another fireball hit the tree near his level sending smoke into his face from the wet foliage. No longer able to see his targets, he hopped down from the tree, stashed his bow on his back, and drew his knives from his belt. He joined the others as they slashed at the wolfbeasts.

As the creatures were defeated one by one, General Morek noticed a clear path to the sorcerer.

Only one spider was still in position to protect him. He charged at the monster, slashing wildly at its legs. It recoiled under the weight of his sword, but its flesh was not cut. The Soulbinder sent a burst of energy directly at Morek, shoving him backwards violently. Striking his head at the base of a tree, he lay motionless on the ground.

Aelryk, seeing his friend was injured, left himself wide open for an attack from an advancing wolfbeast. It slashed his side with its razor-sharp claws before he could turn to face it. Thinal, who was close by, rushed to his aid. She stabbed the monster in its spine, dropping it to the forest floor in an instant.

"My lady," the king said, nodding at Thinal.

She smiled and nodded in response as they both turned to fight two more wolfbeasts. Mel finished off a beast and caught a glimpse of the final spider moving to flank Thinal and the king. He dashed for cover in the tall grass and drew his bow to fire at the beast. In an instant it lay dead, oozing green pus from one eye.

As she slew the final wolfbeast, the sorcerer unleashed his wrath on Thinal. A loud pop filled the air as a lightning bolt hit her in the chest. She dropped to the ground and was immediately encircled in a purple light. Aelryk charged toward the sorcerer. Before he could reach him, the elf toppled from his mount, an arrow sticking out of his eye. His wildcat fled swiftly into the forest.

Mel rushed to Thinal's side and took her in his arms. "You can't leave me," he said, tears welling in his eyes. She was already gone, killed instantly by the blast. He buried his face in her neck and wept. The others stood silently by as Mel grieved for his love.

After a moment, Aelryk knelt next to Mel and placed a hand on his shoulder. "She was a valiant swordswoman. Her death could not have been more honorable." Mel did not respond.

"Shall we prepare a grave for her?" Morek asked, clutching a handkerchief to the wound on his head.

Mel looked up and said, "We do not place our dead in the cold ground. I will place her in the trees as an offering to the sky." He placed her gently over one shoulder and ascended the wide-branched tree nearby. He laid her on her side atop a sturdy branch and placed her hand beneath her head as if she were sweetly dreaming. Kissing her softly on the cheek one last time, he bid farewell to his mate. Silently, he descended the tree.

"I think we may be losing our guide," Aelryk said quietly to Mi'tal.

"I'll track the horses," Mel said as he reached the ground.

The others looked up in surprise. "Does this mean you will stay with us even though your reason for coming along is gone?" Mi'tal asked.

"I promised her I'd see it through," he said flatly.

"I'll come with you," Willdor said. "I'm no physician, but I know some herbs that might help our wounded." He trotted along after Mel, who was barely listening. His heart was far too heavy to think about much else. Thinal was gone, and his world would never be the same.

Chapter 22

"Report," Ulda said sternly.

"Your highness, there was a small uprising in one of the villages," General Fru began. They said they would never accept you as their king and attacked the guards you had posted in their village. Three of them were killed. I immediately led troops to secure the village and have filled your dungeons with those citizens who refused to stop the fighting and swear fealty."

"Well done, General," Ulda replied. "I have need of some prisoners to use as test subjects. My new potion is ready to be tested on humans."

"Shall I have some of them brought up, sire?"

"Yes. Bring four or five of them to my laboratory. Were there any children?"

"Yes, majesty. There were two."

"Bring them as well. I need to test the dosage compared to the size of the subject."

"Right away, my lord," Fru said, bowing. He turned and headed quickly from the throne room.

Ulda rose from his velvet throne cushion and walked slowly to his lab. The potion had worked fairly well on the spiders, but they were still weak at the eyes. The vast majority of Na'zorans fight with swords, so he doubted they would figure out where exactly they needed to stab. They have very few, if any, archers among them which means the spiders should be able to deal more damage than they take. He had already tested his concoction on the wolf hybrids, and they had responded well. They were not indestructible, but their skin was now as tough as leather armor.

Arriving at his lab, he began mixing enough potion to test on his captives. He would start with the highest dose first. If necessary, he would scale it back based on the subject's reaction. Once he had finished mixing, he grabbed his necklace with one hand and placed the other hand on the flask. A pale purple magic surged through the liquid causing it to bubble. He swirled the mixture and held it up to his nose. It smelled faintly of moss.

Just as he was finishing up the potion, the prisoners began to file into the room. Each of them wore chains to prevent them from trying to harm their captor. "Welcome," Ulda said. "Through your disobedience, you have volunteered as test subjects. You will assist me in making my army stronger." He grabbed one of the two children and dragged him closer to his work table. Holding forward a vial full of potion, Ulda said, "Drink every drop."

The boy glared at him and tried to twist out of his grip. Ulda released the child, and shot an energy blast at him. The child dropped to the floor, gasping for air. Ulda grabbed the child's nose, tilted his head back, and dumped the entire potion down his throat. He clapped his other hand over the child's mouth, preventing him from spitting it out. Once he was sure the boy had swallowed, he released him from his grip.

Within seconds, the boy began to seize. He thrashed violently as the other captives cried out in horror. Ulda watched and shook his head. He had a feeling the dose was too high, but the children were more expendable than the adults. He needed adults for mining and to serve in his army. The children, however, were of very little use.

He grabbed the second child, a terrified little girl. This time, he offered her half the amount of potion, and the girl drank it without a fuss. A few seconds passed, and her skin began to glow. Ulda grabbed a knife from his table and slashed at the girls arm. She jumped in fear as the blade struck her, but she was completely unharmed. He smiled at her and said, "Well done, child." She stood motionless, her eyes wide.

He estimated the potion would last up to twenty-four hours before it needed to be readministered. The girl would be monitored by his Soulbinders to test that theory. This process was proving far less expensive and much faster than producing armor for his troops.

Ulda prepared a vial that contained three quarters of the dose that had killed the boy. He offered it to a young male prisoner, who promptly spat in his face. Ulda grabbed the man's throat and unleashed fire with his hand. He did not release his grip until the man's head was nearly severed by the potent, searing magic. The other prisoners stood silently, unable to express their horror at what they had just witnessed.

"You see, I will not hesitate to take your life. You can either serve me and live, or you can die in agony.

It matters not to me, as I can always find someone else to use for testing."

A woman with dark hair extended a chained hand to Ulda. "I will take it," she said. Ulda handed her the vial, and she downed the potion in one gulp. After a few seconds, her skin began to glow. He grabbed his knife and slashed at her arm. She was unharmed. He stabbed the knife into her shoulder, and it sank into her flesh while offering quite a bit of resistance. She gave a muffled cry but managed to endure the pain.

"Excellent," Ulda said. "You now have skin equivalent to leather armor. You are not immune to damage, but you are much less fragile than before."

"Slave!" Ulda shouted towards the door. The boy popped his head inside and bowed. "Have these prisoners taken back to the dungeons. These two ladies will require beds here in the laboratory. Send for my Soulbinders to monitor their progress." He looked down to the floor and added, "Have someone clear away these bodies." The boy ran to obey his master.

Chapter 23

It was late afternoon by the time Mel had located all of the horses. He returned to the camp they had set up not far from where the battle had taken place. Tied to the back of his horse was a boar he managed to take down in the forest.

Mi'tal approached to help him unload the beast. "I hear these things are difficult to hunt, as they can be quite clever."

"Not this one," Mel replied, untying the ropes. "He just stood there and stared at me, so now he's dinner."

Mi'tal chuckled and carried the boar over to the campfire. A good meal was just what they needed after the day's events. Everyone was exhausted, and Aelryk's and Morek's wounds would heal easier if their bellies were full. Nothing, however, could ease the pain in their hearts after the loss they had suffered. Only time could soften the blow Thinal's death had dealt them all.

They ate silently as the waxing moon rose in the sky. The forest was brightly lit under its watchful gaze. From the corner of his eye, Mel noticed a glow near the area where the slain sorcerer lay. Without a word, he stood and went to investigate. Clutched in the dead elf's hand was a small purple gem the size of a duck's egg. Mel picked it up and returned to the camp.

"Any idea what this might be?" he asked, showing the stone to Mi'tal.

"It looks like an amethyst," he replied.

Mel stared at him blankly. Clearly, the word meant nothing to him.

"They're precious gems usually used for jewelry or other ornamentation. It's worth quite a bit of coin."

"Why would a sorcerer be using an amethyst?" Aelryk asked as he came over to look at the gem.

Willdor answered, "Mages can use them as sources of power. Different gems hold properties from different schools of magic."

"Perhaps it was powering his energy attack," Mi'tal said.

"May I see it?" Willdor asked. Mel handed him the gem. "This gem is empty. He may have used up whatever magic was stored inside. Enlightened Elves use magic in a very different way from us humans. I'm afraid I can't be certain what he was doing with this." He gave the gem back to Mel.

Mel shoved the gem into a pocket, and the conversation was over. Having eaten their fill, they settled in for the night. The soft hooting of an owl lulled them to a deep, dreamless sleep.

* * * * *

Two more days of travel brought them out of the woods. They had reached the banks of the Blue River at last. It was very wide and flowed rapidly south. The water was cool and clear with a crystal blue hue. A kingfisher rattled noisily overhead as Mel knelt before the water and drank a handful. It had a sweet, pure flavor to it and was still chilled from its source high in the mountains.

It was mid-afternoon, but the summer's heat was blown away by the cool breeze blowing across the river. "We should camp here tonight," Mel said. "We can get to work building a raft."

"How will we get the horses across?" Utric asked. "It's too deep for them to walk."

"I've never seen a horse float on a raft," Morek said, laughing. The gash on his head was beginning to heal, and he was in much higher spirits than he had been.

"It would have to be a much bigger raft than I'm planning," Mel said. "We'll have to leave them." He thought for a second and then added, "I guess someone can stay behind with them."

"Do you think it's safe?" Willdor asked.

"No, I don't think anywhere is safe," he replied. "You might be alright since you have your potions this time."

"I'm afraid you overestimate my skill in battle," Willdor said.

"Well, how should I know?" he shot back. "I've seen what other sorcerers can do. Maybe you should give that a try."

"That was dark magic," he replied quietly. "I don't practice that kind."

"Let's get started on that raft," Aelryk interrupted. "I don't think any of us want to try to swim with that current."

They busied themselves searching for suitable fallen timber. Mel gathered green vines and began braiding them for lashing. A raft large enough to hold the five of them was going to require a lot of rope to hold it together. Once enough logs had been gathered, the others began braiding vines as well. By nightfall, they had enough rope to attempt assembling the raft.

"Let's get some sleep," Aelryk suggested. "We don't want to cross in the dark anyway. We can tie the logs together in the morning."

No one offered any argument, and they settled in for the night. The air was much more comfortable here since it lacked the heat of the rest of the forest. The sound of the water was very soothing and sleep came much easier.

In his dream, Mel saw Thinal floating on her back in the river. She wiggled her toes to create a splash and giggled as the cool water droplets flew through the air. As he approached the bank, she propped her head up and waved to him. He wanted to go to her and wrap his arms around her, but he could not enter the water. Looking down to his feet, he saw the ground was clear. Nothing was preventing him from reaching her, yet he could not move. When he called out her name, she stood, waved her hand, and turned to leave. Still frozen in place, he tried desperately to break through the unseen barrier. She had already reached the far bank and was fading into the distance. He awoke with a start and looked in every direction. Finally, he realized it had all been a dream, and he remembered that Thinal was gone.

Dawn was approaching, and the forest was beginning to wake. Unable to return to sleep, Mel began tying the logs together to complete the raft. By the time the others awoke at sunrise, Mel was ready to place it in the river. "Let's see if she floats," he said. Aelryk helped by lifting the other side of the raft, and together they placed it in the river.

It sank like a stone.

"Son of a bitch!" Mel exclaimed.

Everyone else stared in disbelief. The raft had not even floated for a second before it sank. Mel knelt next to the bank and placed a hand on the water where the raft had gone in. For an instant, he thought he saw a face in the water amid the ripples. Drawing his hand back quickly, he began to feel very uneasy.

"There's something watching us," he said, sounding rather disturbed.

"From where?" Aelryk asked.

"From the river," he replied.

Aelryk and Mi'tal exchanged glances.

"I thought I saw something, but it's gone. It's just a feeling I guess," Mel added.

"Well, this is a land of fairy tale," Mi'tal commented. "Perhaps there is something more to the water. It may be, your majesty, that you've reached what you seek. We just need to figure out what to do."

"No, Mi'tal," Aelryk replied. "We have not yet reached the Vale. What I seek lies in the land of spring, and it's clearly still summer here. It's cooler, but it isn't spring. We must find a way to cross the river."

Chapter 24

As dawn broke through the Vale, River waded out into the cool waters of the Blue River. He stood at the base of the waterfall and began his ritual of speaking with the Spirit of the river. As always, Lenora stood at the bank to watch.

"Mother," Rogin said as he made his way to the riverbank. "I need to speak with Father. How long until he's finished?"

"It all depends on what he sees in the water. Some days it takes longer than others. You know that, my son."

"There is urgent business, and he is needed. Intruders have set up camp on the far bank. They have just tried to cross the river." Rogin's expression was very serious.

"You cannot interrupt him. If they've tried to cross the river, then he already knows about it. I'm sure he will want to speak with you when he's finished."

"But-," he began.

"Patience, child," she cut him off.

"I'm hardly a child, mother," he replied, annoyed by her remark.

"You'll always be *my* child," she replied. She reached up and kissed his forehead. His demeanor softened somewhat, but his face remained concerned. Impatiently, he stood staring at his father.

Finally, River emerged from the water and dressed. "You bring news, Rogin?" he asked.

"Yes, Father, there are intruders on the east bank."

"I know," he replied. "I have seen them."

"Are they a threat to us? Should we eradicate them?"

River placed a hand on his son's shoulder. "My son, you should not be so quick to fight. Not everyone who seeks our land comes looking for a challenge."

"What are they looking for?"

"Me," he replied. "I will go to them."

"I'm coming with you, then," Rogin said.

"If you must, but they have no weapons that could harm me."

"Would you like me to come along?" Lenora asked.

"I always like it when you come along," he replied, smiling at her. "But I know you have other matters requiring your attention. I won't be gone long." They embraced and parted ways.

River strolled leisurely down the bank followed by Rogin, who did not appreciate the easy pace. He felt pressed to find out what these intruders wanted and would prefer his father not to act so casually. He sighed quietly, knowing that his father would never change. River was incredibly patient and always looked for good qualities in others. Rogin, however, was suspicious of outsiders. These men were trying to reach the Vale, and he did not know their intentions.

They arrived at the bank just across from the campsite. "Wait here, son," River said. Before Rogin could protest, he added, "I will be quite safe." Rogin nodded reluctantly. He gave a low whistle to call some of his troops his direction. He wanted others of his kind nearby in case of trouble.

River dove out into the water and swam gracefully in its depths. He emerged on the east bank, surprising the travelers who had just finished their breakfast. "Greetings," he said as he stepped onto the bank. Despite just having gone for a swim, he and his long blue robe appeared to be completely dry.

Mel stood and gaped at River in amazement. All of a sudden, he dropped to his knees and bowed his head low to the ground, one hand on his heart and the other stretched forward on the ground. "Mistonwey," he said.

River strode forward and placed a hand under Mel's chin, raising his head up to look in his eyes. "Rise, my child," he said. "There is no need to worship me." Mel slowly rose back to his feet, still staring at River.

"Your heart is full of sorrow, Young One. What troubles you?"

Mel remained silent and looked at the ground. He swallowed and felt a lump in his throat. Trying to hold back the tears was useless. He closed his eyes tightly and tried to steady his breathing.

"I see you have lost someone very dear to you," River said. "The wound will not heal quickly, but Thinal's spirit is free. She is at peace. You will find a new purpose in this life."

The others, who had been observing in silence, glanced quickly to each other. This elf did not seem to be a threat, but they could not be sure of his intentions. King Aelryk strode forward to meet him.

"You are the leader of this company," River said. He extended his right arm to the king who extended his own to grasp the elf's forearm. Something about River's grasp gave Aelryk a feeling of well-being. Instinctively, he felt he could trust the elf.

"I am King Aelryk of Na'zora," he said. "May I have your name?"

"No, you may not have that," River replied. "But nearly everyone calls me River. You may call me that as well."

"River," Aelryk repeated. He glanced over at Magister Utric, whose eyes had grown wide at the mention of the name. "I believe I've come here to find you."

"What is it you need of me?" River asked, curiously.

"My people are being hunted by dark sorcerers. A prophecy has lead me to the Vale to find a river. I am supposed to bring him back to Na'zora."

"Indeed, you have found me."

"We tried to cross the river, but our raft sank," Aelryk said.

"That is because you intended to reach the Vale. The river would never have let you cross without permission from my people."

"You control the river completely?" the king asked.

"No," River responded. "The Spirit of the river controls itself."

"You are a servant of the river then," Aelryk said.

"No, I am a part of the river. I will allow you to enter the Vale. Will all of you be coming?"

"Yes, but what of our horses?"

"I will have my son fetch them. He is in need of a task to perform." River seemed amused as he spoke, and Aelryk nodded his approval. River approached the bank where the raft had sank and extended a hand high above the water. Slowly, the raft was drawn up from the depths. "Come along," he said. The others moved toward the bank and began to board the raft. Once everyone was aboard, River waved a hand over the water, and the raft began to move. In less than a minute, they arrived on the west bank.

The air was breezy and cool as they walked through the forest. The trees here were very large and dressed in smooth silvery bark. In front of them lay the elven village. It looked as if the forest itself had conformed to the needs of the elves. They made their homes within the tree trunks whose canopies provided a rooftop. A lush green grass carpeted the entire village. Aelryk had heard tales that they lived among the trees, but this was much different from anything he could have imagined. These were not the savage Wild Elves he had learned to fear in his youth. These were the mysterious Westerling Elves who had not been glimpsed by man for thousands of years.

Chapter 25

River led his visitors to the House of Medicine. They stood amazed as they entered the enormous room.

"How can such a room exist within a tree?" Aelryk asked.

"That is part of the magic of the forest," River replied. "Things are not always as they seem." He motioned for them to follow as he crossed the room. Lenora, who had been busy mixing herbs, turned and wiped her hands on her apron.

"My love, I've brought our visitors to meet you. Two of them are injured and in need of your services." He kissed her cheek and turned to face their guests. "This is Lenora, my life mate. She is the most skilled healer among us. This is King Aelryk of Na'zora and his companions."

"A pleasure to meet you, my lady," Aelryk said.

"My lady," the others echoed.

"It surprises me that you would have much need for healers," Utric remarked. "All of the ancient tales of you suggest you are immune to disease."

"We have little need to cure illness, it's true," she said. "We do get scrapes and bruises like anyone else, and it's a good idea to retain a skill that could prove very useful should the need arise. One never knows what might lie ahead." She approached Morek first and began unwrapping the bandage tied around his head.

"It's much better than it was, my lady," he said as she examined the wound.

"I'll prepare a salve for you. Have a seat there," she said as she gestured to a cot nearby. She looked at the others and asked, "Who else needs treatment?"

"That would be me, my lady," Aelryk said. "I'm afraid I must remove my shirt for you to see it, but I'm not accustomed to disrobing in front of a lady and her husband."

Lenora laughed and said, "I assure you it's no problem." She glanced back at River and smiled. Examining Aelryk's wound, she said, "These scratches are very deep. Was it the same wolf-like beast that attacked the dryads?"

"Yes, it was," River replied.

Aelryk looked at River curiously and said, "How do you know that?"

"I caught a glimpse of the battle when I looked into Mel's eyes. He has a rare gift. Few of the Young Ones still have the green eyes of the forest."

"What does that mean?" Mel asked.

"You have inherited earth magic. Your emerald green eyes are the only outward sign of it. They are very similar to the deep green eyes of the dryads."

"I've never seen a dryad," Mel replied.

"They do exist in your forests, but your people no longer notice them. It takes magical skill to locate them."

"I have no such skill," Mel said.

"You have the ability to learn if you so desire."

Lenora finished applying the salve to Morek and placed a clean bandage over the wound. She created a poultice for the king and placed it over the deep gashes on his side. Delicately, she wrapped a bandage around his torso. "This poultice will help draw out any infection. Whoever treated this earlier saved you a lot of pain."

"That would by my court mage Willdor," Aelryk said. He motioned to Willdor who nodded at Lenora.

"My lady," Utric said. "I don't wish to trouble you, but I am rather old and have not had the easiest time sitting on a horse for travel. Do you have anything to ease the joints of a tired old man?"

"I have just the thing," Lenora said, smiling softly at the elderly man. She walked over to a cupboard and brought out a light pink potion. "Just one sip of this should last you all day," she said, handing him the bottle.

"I thank you, my lady," he replied.

"Perhaps you would like some time to rest," River suggested. "You may stay in my home, and we shall prepare a banquet tonight in your honor. It is long since we had any visitors."

They followed River to his home near the waterfall. The outside appeared to be an ordinary tree of the Vale. It was wide enough at the base for a double set of arched doors and was coated in the same silvery bark. Inside, however, a mansion lay before them. It was spacious and bright with large windows looking out into the forest. The great room window faced the waterfall and framed it as if it were a painting come alive. The walls were etched with scrolling silver branches, and the floor was polished to a high shine.

He led them to a series of doors and said, "You may have your choice of these rooms. I trust you will find them quite comfortable."

"Your hospitality is most appreciated," Aelryk said.

"I will come for you when the feast is prepared. Please, make yourselves at home."

Mel settled into his room, but his mind was whirling too fast for him to rest. Instead, he decided to have a bath. He settled down into the sunken tub in the far corner of his room. His tired muscles were instantly soothed by the warm water, and he dozed for a while in the tub. After some time, he finally felt clean enough to dress. He searched his knapsack for the best clothing he owned and pulled on the tunic and pants. Putting on his boots, he noticed they had apparently cleaned themselves while he was bathing. He supposed it had something to do with the same magic that provided such spacious homes within the trees, and he muttered a quiet "thank you" as he looked around the room.

Exiting into the hallway, he decided he would try to find River. He was curious about the earth magic he mentioned, and he hoped to discuss it further. He checked the great room first and found River sitting on a cushioned bench next to a small girl. She caught sight of Mel and came running up to him.

"Hi, my name's Alyra. What's yours?" she said excitedly.

"It's Mel," he replied. "How do you do, Alyra?"

"I'm doing very well, thank you. Are you one of the Young Ones?"

"I think so," he replied. "At least that's what your father has been calling me."

Alyra laughed and grabbed him by the hand. She led him over to the bench and hopped up on the center seat next to River. Mel took a seat next to her.

"Why don't you go and play for a while, my dear," River said.

"Alright," she replied. "Bye, Mel." She waved a hand at him and trotted down the hall.

"We are the First Ones," River said to Mel. "We are the parents to the Island Dwellers and the Young Ones."

"Island Dwellers?" Mel said. "Do you mean the Enlightened Elves?"

River laughed. "Is that what they're calling themselves now? They've always taken a great interest in matters arcane, so I suppose the title fits. You are a part of our second group of children. That is why we call you the Young Ones. Also, you do not live as long as our elder children, so you remain very young to us throughout your lives."

"That's true," Mel said, "but our lives are very full."

"Is it true you have been mistreated at the hands of the humans?" River asked, sounding very concerned.

"In the past our two peoples have fought over territory. I suppose both sides have done some wrong, but the humans have committed the greater crimes. At least that's my opinion of it. All of that happened before I was born."

"I understand your feelings, Mel. You are quite young and have much to accomplish in your life. I feel strongly that you will help to mend the rift between the humans and the Young Ones." River paused for a moment and then said, "I am so very sorry for the loss of your mate. It is a pain I cannot begin to understand."

Mel remained silent, staring at a spot on the floor. After a few moments of silence, he said, "Can you tell me more about this earth magic you mentioned earlier?"

"You are naturally more attuned to the land and the forests than others. There is magic there, and you could learn to use it. The dryads here in the Vale are friends to us. They could teach you how to use your skills."

"What could I do with such magic?" Mel asked.

"You could do many things, young Mel. You could restore fallen trees and heal their sicknesses. You can learn to communicate with the creatures of the woods. You could even learn to restore the forests that have been destroyed. There are many possibilities, Mel. Those are just a few things you might wish to learn."

"I'm not a scholar," Mel said, shaking his head.

"It matters not," River replied. "You have been born with a gift. If you choose to use it, you will succeed. The dryads can help you learn to channel the magic you already have and bend it to your will. Controlling the gift will take practice and patience, but you will succeed in the end if you so desire."

Mel huffed and said, "I am just a simple elf. It's hard to believe there could be anything special about me."

"You are indeed special, Mel. It's your choice whether you will use your gift to help your people. They could certainly use someone like you."

Mel looked up into River's sapphire eyes and saw pure honesty. He wasn't making a joke, and he wasn't exaggerating. This elf, who he barely knew, could see further into him than anyone ever had. The thought was a little overwhelming. "I think I would like to meet these dryads," he said. "I could at least speak to them and maybe even learn a thing or two."

River nodded. "I can take you to meet them tomorrow. I think they will enjoy speaking with you."

Chapter 26

The banquet was all laid out when River went to fetch his guests from their rooms. He led them to an enormous dining hall where most of the Vale's citizens had gathered for the feast. An elongated oval-shaped table was set at the heart of the room and filled with various savory dishes.

Noticing something was missing, Morek whispered to Mi'tal, "I think they've forgotten the meat."

River, overhearing the comment, said, "Our people do not consume the flesh of other living creatures. I'm sure you'll find some of our dishes to your liking."

Morek nodded. The food before him was very appealing to his eyes, and the mixture of scents were quite tempting. He had no doubt he would enjoy the meal.

River took a seat at the side of the table next to Lenora. He gestured for the king to sit at his other side. Elder Brandor sat at the head of the table. Raising a glass, he said, "My dear elves, tonight we feast to honor the visit of King Aelryk of Na'zora and his friends. We welcome you all to the Vale." He took a sip from his glass as the elves applauded. Aelryk felt honored by their immediate willingness to trust him and his companions.

As the feast began, a beautiful elf maiden played a wooden flute. The music was soft and sweet and carried beautifully throughout the room. Plenty of conversation began among the guests, but the music provided a subtle backdrop to the noise of many voices.

Aelryk sipped from the goblet in front of him and placed it back on the table. "That's quite good," he said. "What is it?"

"It is a wine made from pears," River replied. "The soft flavor goes very well with desserts."

"Ah, I see," the king replied. He took another sip of the wine. "It would go very well with chocolate, I'm sure."

"I've never heard of chocolate," River replied.

"My friend, you have been missing out," Aelryk said. "We will have to remedy that, should you decide to accompany me back to Na'zora."

River smiled and continued tasting the variety of dishes before him. Alyra came running up to him and grabbed his hand. He gave her a quick kiss on the forehead and then hugged her tightly. "My youngest daughter," River said to Aelryk. "Her name is Alyra." She gave the king a cheerful wave and then moved over to speak with her mother.

"Do you have any children?" River asked.

"I have a son," Aelryk replied. "How many do you have?"

"I have seven children," River began. "Three of them are here in the Vale, two have gone to visit the dwarves, and the other two have gone with the river."

"They drowned?" Aelryk asked, his expression concerned.

"No, they cannot drown. Not unless water poured from a glass into a lake drowns. They have traveled far from here, and I have not seen them for many years."

"That must make you sad."

"It does, but I know that they are well. Lenora's mother was against our union because she did not believe I could give Lenora elf children. So far, I've given her five." River smiled and took another sip of wine.

"But you said there are seven," Aelryk said, looking slightly confused.

"Five elves, two elementals. Perhaps more will follow."

"I see," he replied. "And Lenora's father? How did he feel about the two of you?"

"He was very much against it," River said, shaking his head. "He didn't trust me. I think he feared me as many others did when I was young. No one had ever been granted life the way I was, and they did not know my true intentions. With time, they have come to trust and respect me."

"You're quite old, aren't you?"

"Around eighteen hundred give or take a few decades."

"Here I thought I was getting on in age. I seem quite young at only fifty," Aelryk said, laughing. "Your father, does he still live?"

River laughed and said, "We thought he would stay forever, but he finally decided to cross over. He was a member of the Elder Council and truly enjoyed his position. Basically, the council are the eldest among us who are not yet ready to leave. In time, all elves must give their long lives back to nature. It is nature who gives them their existence, and to nature they return."

"You speak as if you are not an elf yourself," Aelryk remarked.

"I am both an elf and a water spirit," River replied.

"An elemental," Aelryk said.

"Yes," River said. "My life belongs to the Spirit of the river. I will not always exist in this form."

Aelryk went silent, lost in his thoughts. He tasted some of the food in front of him and found it very pleasing. The flavors were brand new to him, and he enjoyed the culinary experience.

The elves applauded as the flutist took a bow and left the stage. Lenora ascended the platform carrying a small silver lyre. The elves applauded and then fell silent. She began to sing as she strummed the strings.

At sunrise I heard the voice so clear,
the singing of water, the falls sang with cheer
to herald the morning with chorus of birds.
The sweetest of songs that ever I heard.

How the lights danced on the river so wide.
I longed to stay ever here by its side

and never to part with this River, my love.
Forever my heart would be dreaming of.

I followed the River, my true love and I
from mountain to forest under wide open sky
and all the days long my heart it did sing
Of River and water and the joy it does bring.

My River led on and I did pursue.
Its course ever steady, my love ever true.
Such beauty my River and I did see
the beauties of nature displayed before me.

I love so my River and never would fear
that ever I would part with my River so dear.
At my River's side I would always remain
regardless of challenge or torment or pain.

Still I did follow and never did stray
from my River, my love, I would never away.
We walked ever on, my River and me,
to the edge of the land and the shore of the sea.

The sea! The sea! The gluttonous sea!
It threatens to take my River from me.
A mouth ever hungry, the villainous sea

would swallow my River for eternity.

And into that water the sapphire blue
my River did flow, but I could not pursue.
And here at the shore I shall ever stay
'til my River, my love, shall take me away.

Aelryk joined the others in applause and glanced over at River. His eyes were fixated on Lenora, and Aelryk could see how much in love he still was with his wife of so many years. River stood as Lenora walked back to her seat. Taking both her hands in his, he kissed her long and full on her lips. She blushed a little as they separated and settled back into her seat.

The festivities continued late into the night. By the time Aelryk retired to his rooms, his belly was quite full and his thirst was more than satisfied. These elves certainly treat their guests well, and he was grateful for it. The Vale was, in his mind, a bright spot in a world quickly being overrun with darkness. Tonight he would forget his troubles and sleep peacefully in this fairytale land of spring.

Chapter 27

Tu'vad stood in amazement as he stared at the gold his miners had accumulated in a cellar near the mines. This was a fortune beyond his wildest imaginings. With this gold he wouldn't have to depend on Master Ulda for his livelihood. Next, he would need to take more workers away from the mines to begin refining his treasure. Getting it out of Al'marr in rock form would be far too difficult.

He left the cellar and locked the doors behind him. The mine supervisor was barking orders to his men as Tu'vad approached. "We need to speak," he said. The supervisor nodded, and the pair walked together until they were safely out of earshot of the miners.

"I need workers to begin refining the gold," Tu'vad said.

"Mine production has already been slowed by the search for gold rather than gems. His majesty is going to be angry with us if we aren't providing as many gems as he had hoped." The supervisor seemed very nervous and shifted uneasily as he spoke.

"We'll simply divide up the gems from the other mines and say they're all producing equal shares. He's too busy to investigate further." Tu'vad was smug and very sure of himself. The gold was more important to him than finding gems for Ulda.

"We'll get started straight away, my lord."

Tu'vad turned to leave and began dreaming of the many ways to spend his newfound wealth. Perhaps he would purchase a ship and crew and sail to the Sunswept Isles. He had heard they were beautiful year-round, and the weather was always pleasant. It sounded like a marvelous place to retire from a life of service. He would no longer answer to great men or elves. He would have servants of his own and all the women he could want. Life was going to be very good.

* * * * *

Ulda waited impatiently as the elderly jeweler wheeled in his wooden cart. The old man stopped in front of the throne and bowed low. Ulda moved to the edge of his seat and shouted, "Let's see it!"

The old man removed the cover to reveal the large polished gem beneath it. It was a perfectly smooth oval at least a foot long and six inches wide. The facets caught the light and twinkled before Ulda's eyes.

"It's magnificent," he said as he descended from his throne. He took the stone in his hands and held it close to his face. He gave the stone a kiss and said, "You have done well, master jeweler. You deserve a great reward."

"Your compliments are reward enough, majesty," he replied.

"No, you shall have a real reward. You will no longer live in your workshop. You will be given some of the finest rooms this palace has to offer. When I build my new palace, you will be given a place of honor."

"Thank you, your majesty," the old man replied, bowing.

"You are dismissed," Ulda said.

The old man took the cart with him as he left. Ulda stood fascinated by the gem in his hands. This was the very thing he had needed. He would no longer need to hybridize his entire army. With this stone, he could bind their wills without taking their lives. They would serve him unfailingly and obey his every command. They would no longer think for themselves or their own well-being. He could send them into any battle, regardless of the danger, and they would obey him without question.

"Slave!" he yelled to the boy outside the door.

The pale young boy poked his head inside and bowed.

"Send for General Fru. Have him assemble all of my troops in the courtyard by morning. I need every one of them present."

"Yes, your highness," the boy said, and he ran away down the corridor.

Ulda placed the gem on his throne and headed toward his laboratory. Inside, his Soulbinders were working diligently to create enough of his skin-strengthening potion to distribute among his troops. They stopped as he entered and bowed before him.

"How are the test subjects?" he asked the Soulbinder who was wearing a deep blue robe.

"They have done well, your majesty," he replied. "The girl's potion wore off after about eighteen hours, but the woman's stayed active for almost twenty-five."

"Good," Ulda said. "I am having my troops gathered in the courtyard tomorrow morning. Make sure the woman is among them as well as the others who are in the dungeons."

"Yes, my lord," he replied.

Ulda approached his desk and caught a glimpse of a golden light within his orb. "What could this mean?" he said out loud. He peered into it and realized that the small amethyst he had placed inside the orb contained flecks of gold dust. This could only mean that it had been in contact with gold at some point. "Have any of you been using this orb?" he asked.

All of the Soulbinders denied touching it. Clearly, he was the last to have handled it as his magical imprint was still upon its surface. The jewelers who cut the amethyst were not allowed to handle any other precious metals or gems, so this must mean that one of the mines also contained gold. Gold holds fantastic magical properties and may also be used to bribe their way into Na'zora. He would have to discover which mine contained the gold, and the miners could start collecting that as well.

"Slave," Ulda called to the frightened boy in the corner. "Send for Minister Tu'vad. I have urgent business for him. I shall await him in the throne room. Be quick about it!"

Ulda headed back to his throne room to await Tu'vad's arrival. He lifted the gem again and turned it towards the light coming from one of the massive windows. This was indeed a great prize. The cut was beautiful, and the dimensions matched perfectly with the description in his book. Never before had he held such power, and it was intoxicating.

Tu'vad entered and bowed. "You sent for me, your majesty," he said.

"Yes, I did. I have noticed traces of gold dust on an amethyst in my lab. Find the mine containing the gold and have it extracted."

"I personally inspect the mines every day, my lord. I have seen no hint of any gold," Tu'vad replied. He did not relish the idea of sharing his gold with Ulda.

"I have seen it," Ulda snapped. "You will find out where it is and bring me as much as you can find. Dismissed!" Ulda waved his hand toward the door.

Tu'vad bowed again and turned to leave. Once outside, he took a deep breath and shook his head. Now he would have to split the gold with Ulda, but he had no intention of giving him the lion's share. If he had seen dust, then Tu'vad would offer him more dust and only the smallest pieces. He would keep all the gold that had already been mined, and Ulda could settle for the trace amounts. As long as he was given a small portion, he would never know the difference.

Tu'vad smiled to himself as if he didn't have a care in the world. His day was coming. Soon, he would be his own master with more riches than he had ever dreamed possible.

Chapter 28

It was mid-morning in the Vale as River led Mel to the home of the dryads. The air was cool, and a soft mist fell leaving tiny water droplets dangling from the lush green leaves of the groundcover. A rabbit darted across their path and paused to observe the two elves as they passed.

"These dryads can teach me to use magic?" Mel asked.

"They can teach you to unlock the power within yourself," River replied. "The magic will come with practice, but these ladies can help you to begin."

They halted at a clearing where River sensed the presence of the dryads. A tawny-skinned dryad came forward to greet them.

"Good morning, River," she said, her green eyes sparkling in the morning light.

"Good morning," he replied. "I've brought a friend to meet you and your sisters. His name is Mel, and he would like to learn more about earth magic."

"Indeed," she replied, looking Mel over. "I see he is gifted. Do you wish to learn from us, Mel?"

"I do," he replied.

"Then come and join us." She extended her branch-like arm to Mel. He glanced at River before taking the dryad's hand. "We will keep your friend quite safe," she assured River.

"Thank you, sisters," he said as he turned to walk back to the village. His pace was slow, as he was in no rush to return home. He knew the question that awaited him there, and he wasn't in a hurry to answer it.

Aelryk was waiting outside River's home when he finally arrived back in the village. "May we speak?" Aelryk asked.

"Of course, friend," River replied. They sat together on a silver bench overlooking the river.

"I must tell you the whole reason I am here," Aelryk began. "My kingdom is under attack by dark sorcerers. They are slaughtering my people and carrying others away for some dark purpose. A trusted prophet has informed me that a war is coming, and that I have no hope of defending my people without your help. He told me to travel to a land of spring and bring back the river. That can only mean you."

"I have been aware of this since the morning you first arrived, my friend," River said. "Once you tried to cross the river, all of your secrets were revealed to me."

"Will you come to Na'zora with me?" Aelryk asked.

"Yes, though I do not know how I can help you," River said. "I dislike leaving my home, and I do not do it often. If I alone can save your people, then I must travel with you to your kingdom."

"I am grateful for it," Aelryk said. "Do you have any information about our enemy?"

"I do," River began. "The dryads of the Vale were attacked by those wolf hybrid creatures, and I was able to read their thoughts. They are the bound souls of humans combined with the souls of wolves. I do not know their purpose, but there are few sorcerers capable of such dark magic."

"I have heard tales of Telorithan, who captured the essence of an elemental," Aelryk said.

"Yes, he is quite powerful. However, these beasts came from the sea. I doubt they are under his command."

"Still," Aelryk replied, "I think he may be involved. Do you know where he is?"

"He lives a few hours from here if you travel by the river. If you truly believe he is involved, we could go ask him."

"Is it very dangerous? Would I need to bring an army?"

"Yes, he is very dangerous," River said, "but I would not bring an army. If he feels threatened in the slightest, he will attack first. He's going to see us coming from a long way off. It would be best if only the two of us went to speak with him."

"When can we be off?" the king asked.

"Now, if you like," River replied.

"There is one more thing," he said. He pulled out the purple gem that Mel had taken from the sorcerer who killed Thinal. "The sorcerer we killed in the woods was carrying this. Does it hold any significance?"

"It does," River said, inspecting the gem. "This gem is used to hold the essence of a bound creature. Sorcerers can use it to create powerful enchantments or to supplement their own power."

"It was in the sorcerer's hand when he died. A purple light had surrounded our friend for only an instant before Mel put an end to him."

"Perhaps this sorcerer thought he was powerful enough to bind the essence of an elf. It is a harder task than binding a human, and it appears that he did not succeed." River handed the gem back to Aelryk.

"How do you know?" he asked.

"If there was an essence within the stone, I would be able to communicate with it." River's face was solemn. "Your friend's spirit was not bound. She is free."

"Then let's be off," Aelryk said, sounding relieved. The two of them headed for the bank of the river. Tied to a low tree stump was a long wooden canoe with a scrolling leaf pattern etched into its sides. They stepped inside it, and River extended a hand over the water. The boat began to move forward and flowed smoothly with the swift current toward its destination.

Along the way, Aelryk marveled at the sights of the Vale. The forests were in full bloom, and the sweet fragrance of flowers drifted through the air. Snow-white egrets feasted on fish at the river's edge while swallows darted this way and that to catch tiny insects. A symphony of birdsong provided a subtle but pleasing ambiance.

Time passed very quickly as their boat sped on. Aelryk could tell they had exited the Vale when the heat of the summer began to press down on him once more. The air became thicker, and the forest seemed a little less alive. Fewer birds were singing, and the undergrowth was less disrupted by the movements of tiny, unseen creatures.

River brought the boat to a halt and neared the bank. He climbed out onto the land and tied the canoe to a small tree at the water's edge. Aelryk followed, and together they made their way through the forest.

"It's not much farther," River said. He pointed to a spot above the trees where a tall stone tower was visible in the distance.

A few miles into their walk, a beam of firelight over six feet tall flashed in front of them. When the fire faded away, an elf stood before them. He had long white hair, sun-kissed skin, and bright blue eyes. His face was ageless and very handsome. Aelryk could feel the magical power radiating from this person and knew it could only be Telorithan.

"So you've finally come to subdue me," Telorithan said to River.

"That isn't possible," River replied casually. "The two of us would only make steam."

Telorithan laughed and said, "Then you have no desire to free the elemental? Perhaps you do not love your fiery brother."

"Perhaps fire is vain and needs to learn his lesson," River replied.

Telorithan laughed again. "Why have you come here, and who is this person?" He gave Aelryk a quick up and down look. Clearly, he did not see the king as a threat.

"This is my friend King Aelryk of Na'zora. His kingdom has encountered some trouble, and we hoped you might know its source."

"My people have been attacked and their souls combined with those of animals," Aelryk said.

"It takes very little skill to bind the essence of a human. Your spirits are weak, and your minds are easily controlled. Combining it with an animal is just a fun way of creating a new pet that obeys your every command."

"Are you the one creating these monsters?" Aelryk asked directly.

"No," Telorithan replied, "and I am insulted that you would suspect me. If I wanted your petty kingdom, I would have it. Creating monsters is beneath me, and I have no need of humans as a source of power." He spat on the ground at Aelryk's feet.

"Do you have any idea who might be behind this?" Aelryk asked boldly.

"I do not. I have neither seen nor heard anything."

"We will be on our way, then," River said. "Thank you for taking the time to meet with us."

Telorithan glared in response. Just as the pair began to walk away, River turned and said, "I will come here someday and ask you to release the elemental, but you will refuse."

"Of course I will," he replied.

"I will not be coming alone," River said, and he turned and headed back to his boat.

"How do you know he was telling the truth?" Aelryk asked.

"If he were lying, I would have sensed it," River said. "There was no deception coming from him. He is not the one responsible for the attacks."

The journey up the river was quite smooth despite the strong current. River stopped the boat a few miles away from the village and bid Aelryk to disembark. "We can pick up our friend Mel," River said.

They journeyed a mile into the woods and came to the same clearing where River had left Mel that morning. Mel was seated on the ground with his legs crossed and his hands resting on his knees.

"How was your first lesson?" River asked, breaking the silence.

"Insightful," Mel replied, his green eyes flashing vibrantly. "It begins with the most difficult of simple tasks. Open your heart to the sounds of the forest."

River smiled and nodded. "Once you have accomplished that, you will perform feats of magic you never thought you could."

"I never thought I'd perform any magic at all," Mel replied. "They have also taught me to summon the dryads in the Forests of Viera. They will help me in my training."

"I have never seen any dryads near Na'zora," Aelryk said.

"They are present in every forest," River said. "You've just lost the ability to see them. It takes a special bond with the forest to see into the hearts of trees. Without the dryads, the forests would be gone forever."

Sunset was near as the trio set their feet toward the elven village. The sky was quickly filling with shades of pink and purple, and the dragonflies were buzzing through the air. As they neared River's home Aelryk asked, "When can we set out for Na'zora? I wish to put an end to the evil plaguing my people as quickly as possible."

"I can be ready to leave in two days time," River replied. "I think you will find that time passes a bit more slowly here in the Vale than elsewhere. Your people will risk no greater danger if we stay another day."

Aelryk nodded and headed inside. His heart was hopeful that River could truly bring an end to the attacks and save his people from a great war . He was bringing back the river from the land of spring and fulfilling the prophecy.

Chapter 29

As the sun broke over the horizon of the Vale,

Mel had already made his way back to the clearing where the dryads dwell. The dark of the forest had not posed much challenge for him. With his gift awakening, he could sense the placement of the trees and any other obstacles that were in his path. He had stumbled only once when he strained to see with his eyes instead of with his mind. It took very little to break his concentration, but the dryads had told him that would mend with practice.

He sat at the center of the clearing, meditating deeply. Deep within himself was a small spark. If he could reach it, he could begin to practice his earth magic. For now, finding that spark was difficult. With time, he hoped he would improve. The dryads had said eventually he could do it without even thinking about it. He wasn't sure he would ever get to that point, but he was willing to try. His world had been turned upside down when his mate died, and he longed for a distraction from his grief.

Focusing all of his thoughts inward and breathing deeply, he reached within his own essence. After several minutes, he found what he was looking for. He opened his green eyes, and they flashed with magical intensity. He looked directly at the tree far to his left, and out stepped a silver dryad.

"You are improving quickly, young Mel," she said. She came forward and laid a hand on his shoulder. "Come with me," she said. She led him to the site of the attack on one of her sisters. "Can you feel what has happened here?"

"No," he replied.

"That's because you are only seeing with your eyes and hearing with your ears. What does your heart tell you?"

Mel closed his eyes and took a few deep breaths. Instinctively, he knelt low to the ground and placed an ear close to the forest floor. A moment of silence passed before he sat up and looked at the dryad.

"I see one of the wolfbeasts," he began. "I see a dryad being attacked. She did not survive." He bowed his head in reverence.

"Do you see the damage the beast has done to these trees? We have not yet repaired them, as they were in mourning for our fallen sister. The time has now come to heal them and bring them from their sorrow."

"I don't know how," he said.

"Focus with your heart, and the magic will come."

He moved to the nearest tree and inspected the wounds on its bark. He placed a hand on the wound, bowed his head, and closed his eyes. Nothing happened. Taking a deep breath, he again tried to focus, but still nothing happened. He looked up at the dryad, who was standing patiently at his side.

"I don't know what to do," he admitted.

"Let's sit a while," she replied. Taking his hand, she led him a few steps away from the tree. Together they sat cross-legged on the forest floor.

Mel placed his head in his hands, seemingly defeated. His eyes filled with tears. The dryad placed her delicate hand on his back and said, "It's alright, young Mel. You need to allow your sorrow to flow. You have lost that which is most dear to you, and that wound does not heal overnight."

"Will it ever heal?" he asked.

"You will carry it forever, but it will become easier to bear. You will think of her every day, but it will not always induce tears. Love is a deep emotion, and you can use it to help channel your magic."

Taking her words to heart, he closed his eyes once again and began to breathe deeply. His eyes still shut, he moved to one of the wounded trees. Placing both hands on the wound, he focused his mind to healing the tree. A green glow emitted from his hands. Opening his eyes, he watched as the bark on the tree began to repair. Once it was intact, he removed his hands. He stared wide-eyed at the freshly mended tree.

"Very good, young Mel," the silver dryad said. "You are welcome to heal the others as well."

He repeated the same procedure to heal the five other trees that had been affected during the struggle. When he had finished, he felt light-headed and nearly fell to the ground. Just barely catching himself, he managed to sit softly on the grass.

"The fatigue you are experiencing is your power draining," the dryad said. "That too will change with time. Your magical reserve is low right now, but eventually it will improve. With rest, you will regenerate more quickly each time."

"Does this make me a sorcerer?" he asked.

"You would have to study many different schools of magic for that title to apply. If you stay only with earth magic, you are a shaman."

"I have no desire to learn from the other schools," he replied. "I only want to protect my home in the forest. Maybe I could lead my people back to the old ways when nature was truly revered."

"That is a very noble ambition, young Mel. You have a powerful gift that will aid you in such a task."

Mel ascended into the branches of one of the recently healed trees. "I think I'll rest here a while," Mel said.

"Take all the time you need," the dryad replied. She nestled herself within the hollow of a tree opposite Mel. He closed his eyes and drifted to sleep, soothed by the tranquility of the forest.

A few hours later he awoke with a start. He was drenched in sweat, and his mind was racing. A vision had come to him of the Forests of Viera. He watched as his village was raided by a dark sorcerer and his minions. Many of his clansmen lay dead, and some of them had been carried away towards Al'marr. In a panic, Mel ran to the sleeping dryad.

"The vision, is it true?" he asked frantically.

"It is, but it has not yet come to pass," she replied. "If you hurry, you may still be able to assist."

Without a word, he turned and ran as quickly as possible back to the elven village. He had spent many hours in the forest that day, and the light was already beginning to fade. He hoped River and the king would travel with him, but if not he would travel alone.

Bursting through the doors of River's home, he came first upon Mi'tal. "My village is going to be attacked," he cried, breathing heavily. "We must go and help them."

"We must tell the king," Mi'tal replied.

Aelryk was seated at dinner with River and his family. "You've decided to join us for dinner?" River asked.

"No, my lord," Mi'tal said. "There is an urgent matter to discuss."

"I have had a vision," Mel began. "My village was under attack. The dryad told me I might still be able to help."

"Then we must leave at first light," Aelryk said.

"I will bring my troops," Isandra chimed in.

"This will be no place for a lady," Aelryk replied.

"Just try to stop her," River said. "She is a warrior at heart, and she will not be left behind."

"Very well, then," Aelryk said. "She is your daughter, and you know her far better than I."

"My troops will remain here," Rogin said. "Otherwise there will be no one to protect the Vale, especially if father is going with you."

"Yes, Rogin, you should remain here," River said. "See that our horses are prepared at dawn and waiting for us at the riverbank."

"I will, father," Rogin said.

"It seems the road to Na'zora will be a bit longer than expected," River said to Aelryk. They continued their meal in silence as each of them pondered the events to come.

When it was time to retire, River took Lenora by the hand and walked beside her to their chamber. "It seems I will be leaving you for a time, my love," he said.

"Just be sure you come back to me soon," she replied.

"I will return to you, my love," he said.

They embraced, and he pressed his wife close to his heart. His passion for her was undiminished despite centuries of marriage. She was his soul mate, his light, and his world. They made love long into the night before succumbing to fatigue in each other's arms. The night was silent as the stars closed their eyes, leaving the Vale in darkness.

Chapter 30

As a pale pink dawn broke over the Vale, River hastened his morning ritual. He could not leave without a blessing from the Spirit of the river. Lenora waited on the bank as always, but today her mood was melancholy. Having received the Spirit's blessing, River returned to her. She helped him don a blue and silver robe which she had crafted for him herself.

"I will miss you," she said.

"And I you, my love," he replied.

He took her arm, and together they headed down the bank to meet the others. Alyra came bounding towards her parents, a small gray bag clutched in her hand. "These are for you, Adda," she said, handing the bag to River.

He peered inside and saw a pile of almonds. "To remind you of home," she added.

"Thank you, sweet child," he said. He knelt down and clutched her tightly in his arms. Releasing her, he added, "You must take good care of your mother while I'm away."

"I promise," she said.

Magister Utric walked slowly toward the meeting spot near the bank. "Your majesty," he called to the king. "I request your permission to stay here in the Vale. I am too old to assist in battle, and I would very much like to continue writing my accounts of these marvelous elves."

"Permission granted," said Aelryk. "You will be greatly missed at court. When travel is safe again, I will send a party here to collect your writings. You are most welcome to return at any time you wish."

"Thank you, your majesty," he replied. "I bid you safe travel." He bowed and returned up the bank to the village.

"We are all assembled then," Aelryk said. His own party was joined by Isandra and ten warriors of the Vale. "I don't see any boats to take us across the river."

"Today you will not need them," River said. "You may walk across."

Aelryk glanced back at the water which still appeared to be quite deep. He looked again at River, who smiled and said, "Trust me."

River and Lenora embraced one last time. "Safe journey, my River," she said. He kissed her lips and caressed her face with his hand. Tears filled her eyes as he turned to leave, and she clutched Alyra tightly to her side.

Approaching his horse, a dapple gray stallion with a silver mane, he brushed a hand along its neck. He led the horse across the river as if it were no more than a few inches deep. The rest of his party followed suit, and within minutes, the entire group stood safely on the east bank.

Isandra rode to the front to speak with her father. "Two of my scouts will ride ahead and check for signs of trouble."

"All will be well, Isandra," River said. "I have seen our road."

"Things can change in an instant, Father. It's best to proceed with caution."

"If you insist," he said. "We must travel with all speed."

Mel touched the side of his horse's face. His eyes flashed with green as he tried to convey the need for haste to his steed. The horse whinnied and patted the ground with one hoof. The other horses responded likewise, and the party set off at a thunderous pace.

The forests rushed past as they raced southeast towards Mel's home. As they traveled, a clear path opened up before them. Mel was taking advantage of every bit of skill he had learned in his very short time as a shaman. His desperation to save his clan gave strength to his powers. The scouts had proven unnecessary, as Mel could sense every creature within their path.

They did not pause until late afternoon. There were no signs of water near their campsite, but the horses were tired as were their riders.

"This will just have to do," Mel said. "There are no creeks or lakes within several miles of us."

"The horses need to drink," General Morek said.

"That won't be a problem," River said. He waved a hand over the ground in a circular motion. Water began to pool from the ground until it erupted into a fountain. The horses walked forward one by one to satisfy their thirst.

Mi'tal stared at River in amazement. "How did you do that?" he asked.

"There is water everywhere. I just asked it to join us."

"It is much appreciated," Aelryk said.

There was little time for hunting, so the travelers began eating the trail rations they had brought for themselves. Perhaps the opportunity for better food would present itself later. For now, they were content just to have full bellies.

Mel took a seat next to River and asked, "Do you have the gift of foresight?"

"The Spirit shows me things when there is something I should see," River replied.

"Tell me the truth," Mel said. "Will we make it to my village in time?"

"We will make it in time to save many lives. However, we will not arrive at our destination before our enemy does."

Mel nodded and remained silent.

Chapter 31

Ulda's army of over ten thousand men and elves stood gathered before him in the courtyard. General Fru stood at his side. Ulda had decided it was best not to bind Fru, since he needed the general's military expertise. He didn't want to interfere with military strategies, and Fru's insight may come in useful in battle.

"Soldiers!" Ulda called from his balcony. "You will be the fiercest army Nōl'Deron has ever seen. You will demolish your foes, and you will show no fear!"

The men cheered in response. They had no idea what fate awaited them. For now, they were inspired by their leader and his seemingly glowing compliments of their skill.

"Soon we will set sail for Na'zora," Ulda continued. "We will crush their armies and lay siege to their royal palace. When we have finished, Na'zora and Al'marr will be one kingdom."

Again the crowd cheered. Ulda lifted the oval-shaped amethyst above his head and began chanting as he stared into the gem. His necklace flashed, giving him the extra power he required to accomplish such an astounding feat of magic.

Suddenly, his troops began to feel intense pain throughout their bodies. Many of them doubled over, while others fell to their knees.

Someone cried, "He's killing us!"

Fear spread throughout the ranks. Some of them ran towards the gates, but they had been locked tightly. They were made of thick metal which was nearly impossible to break through, and they were far too tall to climb.

Their fear helped power Ulda's enchantment. It was just the extra boost he needed to facilitate this incredibly difficult spell. As the people below him worked themselves into a frenzy, Ulda continued to chant. A loud boom and a blinding flash emitted from the gem, drawing the attention of the terrified soldiers below. A soft purple light spread over the crowd, and silence and calm overcame them. Ulda had succeeded.

He lowered the gem and clutched it close to his chest. Bending forward slightly, he leaned against the front rail of his balcony. The magical drain was exhausting. Never before had he performed such an immense magical task.

"Are you alright, your highness?" General Fru asked.

"Yes, but I need to rest," he replied. "Send a small group to attack the Wild Elves of Viera. Elven souls will come in very useful when we invade Na'zora."

"Right away, my lord," Fru replied.

Ulda headed back inside to his throne room. He placed the gem on his seat cushion and decided to return to his quarters to rest. Sleep came over him instantly as he lay down upon his bed.

＊ ＊ ＊ ＊ ＊

Morning arrived, and Ulda realized he had slept away almost an entire day. Having regained his magical prowess, he felt rejuvenated. His energy level high, he headed back to his throne room. General Fru was already waiting for him.

"General," Ulda said. "What news?"

Fru bowed before his king. "Your majesty, a small group has been sent to attack the elves as you requested. I have some plans for the invasion ready for your review." He laid a scroll on the small wooden table next to Ulda's throne.

"Is there anything else?" Ulda asked.

"There is one matter, my lord," he began. "It has come to my attention that there is a substantial store of gold being kept hidden from your majesty."

"Yes, Tu'vad is mining some gold for me. So far, he has not reported finding anything substantial."

"My lord, this is a quantity that has already been mined. It is stored within a cellar near the fourth gem mine."

"What are you saying, Fru?" Ulda's eyes narrowed as he scooted forward in his seat. "Are you saying that Tu'vad has betrayed me?"

"Unfortunately, it would seem so," Fru replied. "The miners have been finding gold for weeks now and refining it secretly under Tu'vad's orders."

"Bring him to me," Ulda said flatly.

Within minutes, Tu'vad stood before him. "My lord, how may I serve you," he said.

"You can bring me the gold you've been hiding from me," Ulda said.

Tu'vad glanced at Fru, who raised an eyebrow inquisitively. "There is only the gold I've mined for you, your majesty. Nothing has been hidden."

"Really?" Ulda said. "You haven't had a secret stockpile set aside in a cellar? You didn't order the miners to silence? So far, you have claimed only to find dust!"

"Your majesty, I can explain-," Tu'vad began desperately.

"Guards!" Ulda interrupted. "Take him to my laboratory and have the Soulbinders administer my potion. I will show this traitor what happens to those who steal from me!" He turned to General Fru and said, "I should have known better than to trust the man who betrayed his own king. How could I expect him to be loyal to me?"

"I am sorry, your majesty," Fru said.

"He will never disobey me again," Ulda said. "Have all of the gold melted and we shall dip the traitor inside it. I will bind his will and have a soldier of pure gold. With the souls of a few citizens, I can enchant his golden armor with the strength of steel. He will be my prized soldier."

"As you command, my lord." General Fru bowed and headed straight for the refinery. The men inside were already hard at work preparing the gold to Tu'vad's specifications. "Halt whatever you're doing," Fru commanded. "All of the gold is to be melted down immediately." The workers scrambled to obey.

Having swallowed Ulda's potion without a fight, Tu'vad was dragged into the refinery followed by Ulda. "Please, my lord," Tu'vad shouted. He flailed wildly trying to free himself from the guards.

Ulda began to chant and held forth a medium sized purple gem. As Tu'vad's will came under his master's control, he stopped struggling and stood calmly. "Release him," Ulda told the guards. "He will never again try to escape. Is the gold ready?"

"Yes, your majesty," Fru replied.

"Let's hope my potion is enough to keep this one alive for the procedure. Tu'vad, I order you to bathe yourself in the melted gold." Tu'vad obeyed without any sign of hesitation. The potion did its job to protect his skin, and he was not burned by the molten metal. He emerged, and the metal began to cool.

"Remarkable," Ulda said in amazement. "Now it's only a matter of enchanting the gold. I will have to repair any problems with his movement, and he will certainly need to be strengthened. This may take a few days, but I believe he will be the most spectacular soldier that ever existed." He turned to face his general. "Take him to my lab and have my Soulbinders tend to him," he said. "Oh, and see that five or six prisoners or whoever else is at hand are taken to them as well. They are going to need souls to complete this task."

"Yes, my lord," Fru replied. He hurried to complete his master's instructions. He had seen what became of those who were disobedient, and he had no desire to join Tu'vad in disgrace.

Ulda beamed as he headed back to his lab. His new soldier would make an excellent addition to his army. If nothing else, his very presence would strike terror in the hearts of his enemy. The invasion of Na'zora could not come soon enough. The anticipation induced a wild ecstasy in Ulda.

As he entered the lab, he called out to his Soulbinders, "A golden gift is coming! It is your task to make it useful in battle."

His students bowed in reply. Ulda checked the orb on his table, and noticed a faint blue glow. "What is this?" he asked. He was answered with silence. "No one is using this?"

"No, your majesty," a fair-haired Soulbinder replied.

Ulda peered into the orb, and placed his hands on either side of its smooth surface. Inside, he saw water. It flowed down from the mountains and splashed to the rocks below. For miles and miles it flowed, undaunted by the forests and fields. It sped on until it reached the palace of Na'zora. Ulda looked up from his orb, his face grave. "A water elemental has joined forces with Na'zora," he said. "How is this possible?"

The Soulbinders did not respond. They looked from one to the other and shrugged, not knowing what to say.

"If only I had a large sapphire!" Ulda cried. "I could attempt to bind its essence. What an amazing source of power that would be!" He rushed from the room to visit his jeweler. If only a sapphire large enough could be located, Ulda's chief desire would be fulfilled.

Chapter 32

For days the company journeyed on. Their pace was slowed as the forests of the Wildlands became denser. Mel was able to create safe paths for the horses, but he could do nothing to remedy the tightly packed trees that hindered their passage.

Near sunset, they reached an area next to a small marshland. The cypress trees grew tall, and the scent of wet timber filled the air. The summer's heat lay heavily around them. The marsh flies buzzed past as they sought their dinner, and the mosquitoes whined as they carefully chose the most tender places to bite.

Aelryk slapped at a mosquito as it bit into the back of his neck. The only one who seemed unaffected by their presence was River. "Why don't these little blood suckers like you?" Aelryk asked.

"It's as you said," he replied. "They suck blood, not water."

Aelryk eyed him curiously but swallowed the question that was on the tip of his tongue. Some things were better left a mystery, he decided.

"There's enough dry wood here for a fire," Mel said. "We can throw on some damp logs to create smoke. That will help drive the mosquitoes away."

Though it did not show outwardly, Mel's mind was in deep torment. He knew it was impossible to travel any faster, but he feared how many of his clansmen might lose their lives before he could reach them.

"Do you think there are any edible fish in that pond?" Mi'tal asked.

"I'm sure they would taste awful," Mel replied. "You might catch a frog or two, though."

Mi'tal looked away slightly disgusted. The smell of the marsh combined with the thought of eating a slimy frog did not sit well with his stomach.

Mel harvested some tubers and distributed them among the group. They were crunchy and offered little flavor, but at least they had the freshness that their trail rations lacked.

As evening fell, the noise from the marsh became almost overbearing. The frogs competed for who could sing the loudest, and the crickets chirped incessantly. As the chorus reached a crescendo, Aelryk could no longer ignore it.

"Tell of us the dwarves, Lord River," he said. "A good story will help drive away the noise."

"What do you wish to know?" River asked.

"For starters, I assume they truly exist. You mentioned two of your children were visiting them. To us, the dwarves are as much a fairy tale as you once were."

"They live in the mountains above the Vale," River began. "They're a hard-working, industrious people who mostly keep to themselves. They rarely have dealings with the outside world. Men seldom prefer their mountainous climate, so they are typically left in peace."

"Have you ever visited them," Mel asked.

"Yes, many years ago," he replied. "I was much younger then."

"What are they like?" Willdor asked. "Are they really as unfriendly and boorish as the tales make them out to be?"

"They were not unfriendly to me, but I was able to offer them a bit of assistance. They do not often welcome strangers, but they are not a hostile people." River thought silently for a moment. "They are good people. They live in massive stone halls and enjoy a thick, brown ale. If you are ever given the opportunity to visit with them, I would advise you to take it. I receive them as guests from time to time, and I hope to make the journey to the mountains again someday."

Sunset was swift in the dense forest, and darkness quickly followed. Despite the noise coming from the marsh, the company began preparing their bedrolls in hopes of getting a few hours sleep. River sat alone, looking into the fire. After several moments of trying to find a comfortable branch, Mel gave up and descended from the tree. He joined River by the fire.

"How is your magic progressing?" River asked.

"The dryads seem to think I'm doing well," he replied. "It still takes a lot of effort."

"In time it will be second nature," River said. "You've only just begun to unlock your gift. Patience is difficult in your current situation, but you are not alone in this fight. With a word, you've managed to change the plans of a human king. That's a sort of magic in itself."

"I didn't actually expect him to come," Mel replied. "I hoped your people would send aid, and you have. I never thought any humans, let alone a king, would care what happens to my people."

"Perhaps this king is different," River offered.

"Thirty years ago he led the Na'zoran armies against us. He is responsible for hundreds of dead elves."

"Then perhaps it is time he made amends. We change as we grow older, Mel. You may be too young to understand that, but you are already changing yourself. I doubt you thought you would unlock your magical gifts along this journey."

"I didn't even know I had any magical ability," he said. "I also didn't expect to lose Thinal or that my village would be attacked." From the corner of his eye, Mel noticed movement near the marsh. He looked back at River, who was also looking toward the marsh.

"I've never seen a cypress dryad," River said. "Shall we go and have a look?"

They walked quietly toward the marsh, avoiding the sleeping bodies in their path. Silhouetted in the moonlight, they saw the figure of a dryad crossing the marsh. Aware of their presence, she changed directions to greet the pair. She moved silently, despite being ankle deep in the murky water. Her reddish-brown skin was covered in patches of bright green moss. Her hair was silver and reached far below her waist.

"She's beautiful," Mel commented.

River nodded and replied, "She is a guardian of the woods. You are a shaman, her kinsman."

She approached the pair, and a warm smile spread across her face. "Welcome, Mel," she said. "It is an honor to meet you." She extended a hand to him. "Lord of Waters," she said, nodding to River in acknowledgement.

"Good evening, my lady," he replied.

"What brings you two here?" she asked.

"We are returning home from the Vale," Mel said. "My people are in danger."

"That is troubling news," she replied. "Please have a seat." She gestured to a fallen log.

A mist began to settle over the marsh. The particles flashed as they caught the moonlight. They shifted and swirled in some exotic dance despite the stillness of the air. The lightning bugs floated lazily above the mist, flashing their yellow beacons carelessly.

"Your mind is troubled," the dryad said sympathetically.

"Yes," Mel replied.

"I think I have something that can help you." She rose and headed back into the marsh, disappearing inside a cypress. When she emerged, she held a small pouch in her hands. "The heartwood of a cypress," she said. "This will ease your burden, and your magic will flow more freely." She hung the pouch around his neck with a small string of beard moss.

Mel immediately felt its empowering effects. His weariness faded away, and he felt as if he had already had a good night's sleep. "I'm most grateful to you," he said, touching his hand to the pouch.

"We are creatures of the forest," she replied. "We must stand together in times of need. Call on the dryads of Viera. They can help you." She headed back out into her marsh, turning once to wave goodbye to her new friends. The mist thickened, and she disappeared within the dense cloud. River clasped Mel on the back, and the pair returned silently to camp.

Chapter 33

At dawn the company once again mounted their horses and proceeded hastily to the Forests of Viera. Mel's heart was still burdened, but the dryad's gift had filled him with hope. Each step brought him closer to his homeland and saving the lives of his kin.

As they pressed onward through the heat of the day, Mel projected energy to invigorate the horses and give them the stamina to continue. Though domesticated, their ancestors had roamed freely through the Wildlands. He tapped into the untamed spirit that still dwelt deep inside the noble creatures.

At mid-day the sun's heat was oppressive. The company was forced to stop for fear of overheating the horses. River produced another fountain to provide drink, and lifting his face towards the sky, he called down a gentle mist to cool his companions. It felt as soft and cool as the rain in the Vale. It was a very welcome relief for the weary travelers.

The following morning offered much-needed relief in the form of cloud cover. The sun's rays were blocked, and the riders continued more comfortably than they dared hope. Mel's village lay just ahead. As they approached, cries could be heard in the distance, and smoke was rising over the tree line.

The Westerling Elf troop headed to the front and took on a charge formation. Isandra led the way as they galloped into the village. Two sorcerers mounted atop wildcats commanded more than thirty wolfbeasts and at least twenty spiders. Elves were running through the village to get to their weapons. A few of them were already fighting, and those who could not fight were fleeing in a panic.

Isandra's troops made short work of four wolfbeasts as they rode over them, crushing them beneath their horses. Still mounted, she swung her sword at an attacking spider and quickly realized it was armored. Her sword could not penetrate its tough flesh. She drew a small, pointed dagger and hopped down off her horse. Instantly, the spider grabbed her and flung her on her back. Its massive pincers snapped wildly as she grabbed them with her hands. Drawing her legs up, she kicked the spider solidly in the abdomen. It bowled over, and she sprang on it, stabbing deep into an eye. It hissed with pain as she proceeded to stab a second eye, this time leaning her full weight against the dagger. Finally, the spider stopped moving, and its legs curled inward.

"Are you alright?" one of her troops called to her.

"I'm fine," she replied, "but I could use a longer dagger."

River had ridden further into the village where a group of children and elderly had sought refuge from the sorcerers' fireballs. They were huddled behind a group of huts that had not yet been touched by the flames. Spreading his arms out before him, he raised a shield wall of water to protect the frightened elves. The children were hypnotized by the shimmering blue water, and their fears were quelled.

Upon seeing the shield wall, both sorcerers decided to take on the challenge. They focused their energy toward River and sent out blasts of lightning in his direction. The light hit the shield wall and was consumed by it. The shield glowed brighter, invigorated by the infusion of magic. Dismayed, the sorcerers unleashed a second energy blast at the shield. Again, the shield drank their magic and strengthened itself.

A spider was commanded to attack the shield and scurried quickly toward River. As soon as it reached the wall, its black skin began to melt. Within seconds, it was only a small black puddle that was quickly lapped up by the shield wall.

River stood steadfast with all of his concentration focused on the shield protecting the villagers. One of the sorcerers charged at the wall. He conjured a shield bubble of his own in an attempt to protect himself from the water. Drawing his staff, he pointed it at the wall and unleashed a magical blast. The force knocked him from his mount, and he struck the ground roughly. A volley of arrows from the trees finished him off before he could regain his footing.

Aelryk fought alongside Morek and Mi'tal. With their backs together they were able to slash through the ranks of the savage beasts as they approached from all sides. The elves once again reformed the line and charged toward the monsters. The trio dodged expertly to the side, allowing the charge to hit its mark. Wolfbeasts lay bruised and broken on the ground. They had grown much tougher and more resilient since their last encounter with them. Many of them survived the charge but were badly wounded. With a nod of gratitude to his elven comrades, Aelryk began slicing off heads to ensure the wounded beasts would not recover.

Mel had taken to the trees and was firing arrows at the eyes of the spiders. They were very small targets, and the spiders were in constant motion. Some of his clansmen had taken to the surrounding trees which made it possible to attack them from different angles. Together they brought down the majority of the spiders. Those whose eyes they could not hit were driven by volleys of arrows into River's shield wall. Before long, the spiders were no more.

The monsters having been dealt with, River released the shield wall and threw it around the remaining sorcerer. He wanted to speak with him and find out who was behind the attack. His mount reared, throwing the sorcerer to the ground. In a panic, it began running in circles. The elves stayed their arrows as Mel descended from the trees and cautiously approached the animal. He extended a hand towards it, and the cat backed away slowly. A flash of green from Mel's eyes released the wildcat from its spell of bondage, and it bounded away into the forest. It looked back at him and lowered its head in gratitude.

River, Aelryk, and Mel approached the trapped sorcerer where he still lay on the forest floor. "Who sent you here?" River asked.

The Soulbinder only shook his head, refusing to speak to them.

"Remove the shield and I'll beat it out of him," Mel said.

River reached his hands through the shield and placed them on each side of the sorcerer's head. The Soulbinder's eyes went wide, and his neck muscles tensed. Closing his eyes, River began to speak. "Master Ulda of Ral'nassa has taken over the kingdom of Al'marr and is using human souls to power his enchantments and create these beasts. They were here hoping to trap elven souls to power even stronger enchantments. Soon, Ulda plans to invade Na'zora and take it for himself. He also plans to attempt binding the essence of the water elemental that has allied itself with the Na'zoran king. That is all he knows."

River removed his hands from the sorcerer and dropped the shield wall. Without a word, Mel drew one of his knives and cut the Soulbinder's throat. Turning, he looked upon the destruction of his village. Many huts had been burned, and the bodies of elves lay dead on the soft grass.

Willdor began gathering the wounded together to better assess who was in most urgent need of treatment. "Where is your village healer?" he asked one of the wounded elves.

"He is dead," the woman replied. "He was the first to fall."

Mel remembered the words of the cypress dryad. He closed his eyes and projected all of his energy to summoning the dryads of Viera. Though he had never seen them, he knew they were near. His focus began to wander, and he clutched the small pouch containing the heartwood in his right hand. His resolve strengthening, he reached deep within himself and called out with his heart.

Gasps came from the stunned villagers as four silver-skinned dryads emerged from the forest. Each was carrying a wooden platter filled with medicinal herbs. They walked gracefully into the village and began to tend to the wounded elves. Willdor stood a moment enraptured by their beauty but finally managed to regain his composure. He offered his assistance to the ladies, who gladly accepted.

Aelryk looked at River and said, "Do you know when he will invade my kingdom?"

"The sorcerer only knew that it would be soon."

"And binding the elemental," Aelryk began. "That means he's aiming for you next."

"I should prove a most difficult target," River said. "Do not worry about me."

Mel's face was beginning to show the signs of his fatigue. "We have a lot of rebuilding to do here. Our overseer has been killed in the battle, and my clan is in need of strong leadership. I will not be coming with you to Na'zora. I'm needed here."

"I understand," Aelryk said. "You have fulfilled your promise and more by leading us safely to the Vale. I am in your debt."

Mel replied, "You are all welcome to stay here as long as you need. We are all very grateful for your help. Many more would lay dead if you had not come with me." He nodded at River and rejoined his clansmen at the center of the ruined village.

Chapter 34

The rest of the day was spent clearing out the ruined huts and rebuilding them to provide adequate shelter for the elves. Many of them would still have to spend the night in the trees, but their homes could be repaired in a matter of days. The structures were simple but sturdy.

Mel personally attended to his fallen clansmen. He carried each body safely into the forest and placed it in the limbs of the surrounding trees. The birds would scatter them to all corners of the Wildlands, and they would again rejoin the forests who birthed them.

It was a somber task which he did not enjoy. With so many others injured, and the rest busy rebuilding their homes, Mel felt it was his duty to tend the dead. They had been the village's first line of defense, fighting unarmed to slow the invasion of the monsters while the others retrieved their weapons.

Once all of the fallen had been tended to, Mel went to check on the wounded. The dryads were still busying themselves treating them, and he wanted to offer his help. Even before he discovered his magic, he knew a lot about the herbs available in the Wildlands. He was no healer, but he knew which plants would help seal a wound and prevent infection.

"Do you ladies need anything?" Mel asked one of the dryads.

"We have enough of what we need for now," she replied. "You look like you could use some rest."

Mel shook his head. "I just haven't had a moment to clear my head."

The dryad placed a warm hand on Mel's cheek. "Your people need you now more than ever. If you are to be strong for them, you must take care of yourself."

"I will," he replied.

She handed him a small bundle of leaves and said, "Eat this. It will make you feel better."

Mel obeyed. The leaves had a bitter taste, but he chewed them until they were nearly gone before he swallowed them. Despite the flavor, they provided a very soothing feeling in his stomach. Most of his tension drained away, and he was able to breathe more freely. Perhaps he would take a few moments for himself to meditate in the forest.

He traveled only as far as the edge of the village and sat cross-legged with his back against a tall silver tree. Closing his eyes, he allowed his mind to wander. An image of Thinal came to him. She was sitting beside him beneath the green canopy of the forest. She smiled her usual happy smile. It would seem the devastation of their village had not dampened her spirits. Ever the optimist, she projected joy wherever she went. Death, it seemed, had not affected her happiness.

Opening his eyes, he looked to his side and saw nothing. She had not really been there, of course, but he had sensed her presence very strongly. Staring up at the sky, he watched as birds darted back and forth through the trees. They too had been unhindered by the fighting below. They could overcome anything by flying to a new home if the old one became unsuitable. Mel did not have that option. His people would stay and rebuild their village. Their wounds would heal, and the forest would take care of them.

* * * * *

"Father," Isandra said. "Will the village be safe if our troops head to Na'zora?"

"Mel will be able to sense any further danger. The forest will warn him, and the warriors here are brave and strong. They will not be taken by surprise again." River spoke with assurance. "This Master Ulda is going to be very angry when he sees what happened here, and he is too smart to risk attacking this village again. It is Na'zora that is going to need protection now."

"I'd like to leave first thing in the morning," Aelryk said. "It's a day's ride to the border from here and another day back to the palace."

Both Isandra and River nodded their agreement.

"We will ride through the village of Enald. I will have the townspeople send supplies to aid these elves." Aelryk turned to have another look at the devastation. "Do you think they were able to bind any of the elves' spirits?"

"No," River replied. "The fallen were killed too quickly, and they did not make any attempt at it once we arrived."

Aelryk lowered his voice to nearly a whisper. "Can you be so sure?"

"I examined the gems taken from the sorcerers' bodies. They were all empty."

"What do you think has become of my citizens who were taken? Do any of them survive?"

"They are most likely dead," River said solemnly. "I believe they have all been used in creating the hybrid monsters. He wanted the elven souls to power his enchantments. They would have lived indefinitely in torment with their spirits trapped inside those gems."

"I can't say which fate is worse," Aelryk said, shaking his head. "I'm going to join the hunting party. Maybe we can find these people something good for dinner."

River and Isandra headed into the woods to find Mel. He had drifted off to sleep beneath the shade of a birch tree. As they approached, he awoke and looked up at them. "I guess I fell asleep," he said.

"It's been a long day," River replied.

Mel stood and stretched his neck to either side. "Has any progress been made in my absence?"

"Yes," Isandra said. "Four huts have been rebuilt, and they're working on a fifth."

"I guess I should get back to work, then," he replied. "How long are you staying?"

"We leave in the morning," River replied.

"Do you suppose I'll ever see you again?" Mel asked.

"I doubt I shall travel this way again, but you are always welcome in the Vale."

"I'd like that," Mel said, smiling. "That is, if I ever get another opportunity. Some of my clansmen are saying they want me to be overseer."

"You don't want the title?" Isandra asked.

"I'm usually the guy who tells the overseer when he's being an idiot," Mel replied. "I'm not used to being the person in charge."

"You're a shaman, Mel," River began. "Who is better to lead your people? They need your guidance now more than ever. Your path in life is much changed."

"I guess it is." He watched as his clansmen continued working on a hut. They were so distracted by their work that he wondered when the grief would set in. A period of mourning would need to be observed in respect for those who were lost.

The hunters began returning bearing fruit and nuts. King Aelryk returned with an elk, and the elves gathered to prepare it for dinner. Their spirits were high as they cooked and ate, and Aelryk admired their resilience. This was no savage race of elves. In fact, he found them to be very much the same as his own citizens.

"We give thanks to the forest for providing this feast before us," Mel said. "We also give thanks for the lives that were spared and for the help of our friends from the Vale and Na'zora."

The villagers cheered in reply.

"We also honor those who gave their lives to defend our homes," he continued. "Once our village is restored, we will mourn for them properly."

Many of the elves nodded and spoke softly to each other. They had pushed the thought from their minds, but the sorrow had touched their hearts. Their clansmen would not be forgotten.

Chapter 35

Ulda marveled at the extraordinary work his Soulbinders had done. Not only had they strengthened Tu'vad's golden armor, they had increased his height and bulk. He was now even more intimidating. "He's magnificent!" Ulda cried. "You've done very well, my students. This exceeds my expectations."

His students bowed their heads before him. Compliments rarely came from Ulda's lips, so they tried their best to enjoy the moment.

"One of you must take control of him," he said. "Which one of you would like the privilege?"

The students looked at each other with excitement. They were all most eager to please their master, and they all wanted this chance to prove their worth. All of their hands shot into the air as if they were impatient school children.

Ulda laughed. "Only one of you can be given this honor. Who has done the most work in transforming him into this work of art?"

A Soulbinder in a black robe stepped forward. He had a long crooked nose and close-set eyes. "Your majesty, I am responsible for his increase in size. I created the enchantment using the essence of a rather large prisoner. We all contributed to the enchantments, but that one was my idea."

"Well done," Ulda said. He handed the gem containing Tu'vad's essence to his student. "He was a skilled fighter, but it will require all of your concentration to control him. He's just a giant lump of metal now, and he won't think for himself. I don't want to see him standing idly on the battlefield."

"Yes, my lord," the Soulbinder replied.

"The rest of you will be responsible for leading our hybrid army. General Fru will familiarize you with the battle formations and strategies he wishes to use. Listen to him. He is a decorated general, and he has served me very well."

"When are we leaving, your majesty?" One of his students asked.

"We will begin loading the ships in three days time. Then it's up to the wind how quickly you arrive in Na'zora. I will not be traveling with you, but I will be monitoring your progress from here. My orb will show me everything."

The Soulbinders bowed as Ulda left the room. He headed for his throne room to speak with General Fru. "How are the preparations coming?" he asked as he crossed the room to take his seat.

"Very well, your majesty," Fru replied. "We have five ships ready to take us up the coast to Na'zora. Three ships will hold your human army, while one will carry your Soulbinders and their minions. At your request, one is being left behind for your personal use."

"Good," Ulda said. "I'll need it to join you quickly once you've secured the kingdom. What preparations have you made in case they don't want to come out and fight?"

"There is plenty of room for supplies in case of a long siege, your majesty. I don't think it will be an issue with the Soulbinders along. Their lightning and fireballs won't allow the king of Na'zora to hide for long. We'll have his walls down in no time."

"Has there been any news of the party that was sent to attack the elves? We need those souls brought to us quickly if we're to prepare them."

"There has been no word of them, sire," the general replied. "If they were successful, they should be on their way back by now. If they don't arrive by tomorrow evening, we must assume they have failed."

"It's possible the elves were forewarned of the attack. Has there been any luck in locating sapphires?"

"None of any significant size, my lord. My troops are still conducting searches."

"See that they are very thorough. This could be my only chance. If you manage to subdue the elemental, it must be brought to me immediately. Do not kill it under any circumstances. Use any means necessary to contain it, but it must remain alive if it's to be of any use to me."

"As you command, my lord."

"Do you find my army more eager to serve since their binding?"

"I do, majesty. They are very quick to follow my orders, and I have no doubts they will serve you well in battle."

"Fear is no longer a consideration for them," Ulda said proudly. "They are a masterpiece."

"Indeed, my lord," Fru replied. "It is a rare treat to have troops so passionate. They think only of the upcoming battle and how they may serve."

"Excellent," Ulda said, clapping his hands together. "Everything is prepared then."

"It is, sire," Fru said. "Na'zora will be yours."

"I'm counting on it," he replied. "Once you've gained control you will have to keep everything in order until I arrive."

"It will be an honor, majesty."

"You're dismissed."

As the general left the room, Ulda began to ponder the possibilities once he held Na'zora. It was a far larger kingdom than Al'marr, and more citizens meant more souls for testing. He would be closer to several clans of Wild Elves, and with his new Na'zoran army he would make quick work of capturing and binding them.

Then there was the small matter of binding an elemental. If a water spirit was available for the taking, he did not want to miss the opportunity. He may have to turn all of Nōl'Deron upside down to find a large enough sapphire, but that was a challenge he was most willing to undertake.

Chapter 36

A cool morning arrived in the Forests of Viera.

The wind was sailing through the trees reminding everyone that autumn was finally approaching. King Aelryk and his companions were glad to be traveling in these improved conditions.

It would take the better part of a day before they reached Enald. Aelryk hoped the town was still standing since his absence. He did not know how many attacks may have taken place on his people while he was away. If the village still stood, they would rest there for the night and then press on for the palace. The majority of his army was stationed there, and they would need to be prepared for the upcoming battle.

As they approached Enald from a distance, they could see that the village was intact. A wave of relief came over Aelryk. "We will stay here tonight," he announced to his companions. "We will leave at first light and reach the palace by nightfall."

Enald had no buildings large enough to accommodate the entire group. Instead, the travelers put together a make-shift camp at the edge of town. They would be in position to protect the village should another attack take place.

"General Morek," Aelryk said. "We need to ready scouts to discover where Ulda's armies are heading. We don't have enough men to protect all of our borders."

"That won't be necessary," River interrupted. "They will approach from the sea."

"How do you know that?" Morek asked.

"It's only a day's ride from here to the sea. I can hear it."

Morek and Aelryk exchanged glances. River could be vague at times, but they trusted his counsel.

"Then we will focus all of our attention to the sea," the king replied. "I will dispatch a messenger to ride through the night and alert my councilors. They can begin preparations for war."

The citizens of Enald began wandering into the king's camp. They had never seen such elves before, and many of them wanted to take a closer look. The

Westerling Elves had an aura of peace and goodness about them. Their steadfast hearts projected a positive energy to the villagers. Their hearts filled with hope as they looked upon the mysterious elves of legend. A fairy tale had come to life to save them in their hour of need.

As the night set in, Aelryk was filled with anxiety and falling asleep was impossible. He did not know how long he had until Ulda's forces arrived. They may even be attacking now. The thought weighed heavily on the king's mind.

At dawn he asked River, "What does the sea say to you? Are my people already under attack?"

"Ulda's men are still preparing their ships. They have not yet left Al'marr."

Aelryk closed his eyes and breathed out heavily. The burden in his heart was lifted. He knew now that he would arrive in time.

They galloped along the road that would lead them at last to the king's palace. Villages came and went as they hurried past. At the sight of their king, many citizens would cheer and wave. Aelryk had no time for fanfare and could not spare a moment to greet them. They carried on throughout the day and reached the palace just as the moon was ascending in the sky.

Servants flocked to them taking their horses and helping unpack their gear. Upon entering the palace, Aelryk began issuing orders to the servants. "Find rooms for our guests from the Vale and inform my councilors that there will be a meeting at dawn. Have all my lieutenants in attendance as well. Tomorrow, we prepare for war."

Lisalla had been told that her husband had arrived home at last. She quickly descended the wide staircase leading to the palace entrance. "My king," she cried, rushing to be at his side. "It is good to see you."

"I have missed you as well," he replied. "May I introduce you to Lord River of the Westerling Vale and his daughter Isandra."

"A pleasure," she said.

"My lady," River replied.

"I presume you are the river that my husband was charged with finding," she said. "I am happy you have come."

"As am I, my lady," he replied.

* * * * *

The following morning, Aelryk's councilors and lieutenants gathered within the council chambers to discuss preparations for war. They were all assembled as Aelryk arrived followed by River and General Morek.

"Good morning, my lords," the king began. "Today we must discuss an invasion fleet that is on its way from Al'marr as we speak. Master Ulda of Ral'nassa has taken control of that kingdom and has set his sights on Na'zora as well. He must be stopped at all costs."

Murmurs flew from the councilors lips as Aelryk continued to speak.

"We must have our armies prepared to meet them on the beaches. Our smiths will be working overtime to ensure our weapons are in good repair. Have every man examine his weapons and armor immediately to determine which pieces need repair. There is no time to waste."

"Majesty," Loren began. "Could we not wait them out in the palace? They will never get through our walls. Surely they would give up and return to their homes."

"They have an unknown number of sorcerers with them. Our walls will not stand long under their concentrated fire. Draw up your plans, gentlemen. I will return this afternoon to go over them."

He headed towards the door and spoke to River, who was seated nearby. "Come with me."

River followed the king out the door and into the marketplace. They headed for the armory where Yori was hard at work. Apprentices were running back and forth with various pieces of equipment. Yori stopped working at the sight of his king. He stood, and his eyes locked on River.

"Yori, this is Lord River of the Westerling Vale. He'll be needing some armor forged. I trust you can handle it quickly."

"Of course, your majesty," he replied, still staring at River. "What are you?" he finally asked.

"An elf," River replied.

"You're much more than that," Yori said. "You are one of the First Ones."

"I am."

Realizing that he was still staring, Yori shook his head. "Forgive me. Let me take your measurements for the armor." Taking each measurement twice, he jotted the numbers down on a small piece of parchment. "What kind of runes do you require on your armor, my lord?"

"None," River replied.

Yori opened his mouth to say something, but the words did not come.

"You'll want some enchantments, River," Aelryk said.

"It isn't necessary," he replied. "I am my own enchantment."

"I knew it," Yori said. "You are an elemental."

"Correct," River said, smiling. "It wasn't meant to be a secret."

"Your eyes gave it away," Yori replied. "I just had a feeling when I looked at you. Without any special runes, I can have this completed in two days. I'll make this my top priority."

"Thank you, Yori," River said. Yori nodded in acknowledgement.

"Come, Lord River," the king said. "There is something I must show you."

They headed for a booth in the marketplace that was selling honey and dried fruits. The short, dark-haired merchant bowed at the sight of his king and greeted him with a nervousness in his voice.

"Greetings, your majesty," he said. "How may I serve you today?"

"I hope you have some chocolate, my good man," Aelryk said.

"Yes, your majesty," the merchant replied. "It's nothing special, though, just melted chocolate. It's been far too hot to keep any fine chocolates on hand."

"Melted will do just fine," the king replied.

The merchant filled a small bowl with the warm, sweet chocolate and handed it to the king.

"Do you have any of those almonds left?" he asked.

River produced the small pouch Alyra had given him.

"Dip one in the chocolate and taste it. You've never experienced any taste so divine."

River did as the king suggested. Upon placing the chocolate coated almond in his mouth, his eyebrows shot up in amazement. "It's delicious," he said. Licking the chocolate from his fingers, he added, "This is the best thing I've ever tasted. Thank you for sharing it."

Aelryk laughed and nodded. He clasped him on the back and handed him the bowl. "Enjoy it, my friend."

"I will," he replied, munching on another almond. "Could I have a look at the ocean? I've rarely been this close to it."

"Certainly," Aelryk said. He led the way down to the beach just behind the palace. As they neared,

River stopped suddenly and recoiled as if he had been struck.

"Are you alright?" the king asked as he helped to steady his friend.

"I'm fine," he replied. "It's just that there are so many voices in the sea. It's a little overwhelming at first."

"Voices?" Aelryk asked, wrinkling his brow in confusion.

"All rivers empty into the sea eventually," he began. "There are millions of river spirits here, and they all speak at once. It's difficult to focus on just one."

Aelryk looked out over the endless blue sea. It spread towards infinity, where the blue of the water met the blue of the sky. He heard nothing except the whistle of the wind and the crashing of the waves.

River walked towards the blue water as if hypnotized. He stood in the foam deposited by the waves and closed his eyes. The voices grew louder and softer as the spirits danced about in the ever-changing water. He reached out with his mind to speak with his watery brothers and sisters. Some were near and others far. In the distance, he could hear the sound of Ulda's ships still being prepared for battle in Al'marr. They were nearly ready to depart. In a few days time, Na'zora would be at war.

Chapter 37

Yori waited in the palace foyer with the newly crafted armor. He stood patiently as a servant ran down the long stone corridor to fetch River. There seemed to be a chill inside the palace that day despite the summer weather outside. An anxious mood permeated throughout the structure as the kingdom prepared for war.

River appeared in the foyer and offered a hand to Yori. "It is most kind of you to bring this here. I could have easily come to you. I know you are terribly busy."

"It was no trouble, my lord," Yori replied. "I like to personally perform the final fitting. It's the only way to ensure it's done properly."

"Very well then," River said.

The pair headed toward River's chambers where Yori began laying out the various pieces of armor. He sat each piece carefully on the bed for River to inspect. Each piece had been tinted sapphire blue in color. It had a radiance unlike any other armor Yori had created. He had spent many years working for the king and had created some very special pieces on his behalf. This work, however, was something entirely different. This piece was suitable only for an elven lord of great power. Yori had taken immense pride in crafting it.

"This is exquisite," River remarked. "This must have taken a vast amount of work."

"It was a pleasure," Yori replied. "It's not often that I get to craft armor for a member of my own race, especially one of your standing."

"It must have been difficult being a child of two worlds," River said. "Have you spent much time among your elven kin?"

"They are the ones who taught me the runes," he replied, "but most of my life has been spent among humans. My father was a member of the Sycamore Clan, but he was killed when I was very young."

"I'm sorry to hear that," River said. "You seem to have done very well for yourself here in Na'zora."

"Yes," he replied. "The king and I are friends. I'm not sure where I'd be without him." He began buckling the armor onto River. The fit was perfect, and the color suited him well.

"It's lighter than I expected," River observed.

"Yes, my lord. You did not ask for any enchantment, but I always etch runes that reduce the weight of my pieces. It keeps the wearer moving freely and reduces fatigue."

"I am most grateful for it," River replied. "I am not used to wearing such things as this."

"It suits you," Yori said.

"You should visit the Vale someday. You could exchange knowledge with our smiths. I'm sure they would enjoy your visit."

"I would love to," Yori replied.

Just then, a rapid knock came from the door. A young page stuck his head inside and said, "I'm sorry to disturb you, my lord. The king has asked for you to come straight away. The ships are approaching."

"We can speak more later, Yori. Thank you."

River followed the servant to meet Aelryk. He was standing on the balcony just outside of his council chambers, his eyes fixated on the sea.

"They've arrived," he said without turning around. "The battle is about to begin." He turned to River, who was looking solemnly at the ocean. "I see Yori has already prepared you. May that armor serve you well."

Together they proceeded to the palace courtyard where the army was assembling. Isandra and her elven comrades were already prepared for battle and awaiting further orders. "Father," she said, as she saw him entering the courtyard. He approached her and gave her a kiss on the cheek. "The enemy is almost upon us," she said.

"I will lead the first attack myself," Aelryk said. "General Morek, your company will follow mine as we discussed. We must stop as many of them as we can before they reach the palace."

"I'd sell my own mother for a dozen archers right now," Morek replied.

"I guess that means I'm just in time, then," Mel said.

Stunned, Aelryk and Morek watched as Mel approached followed by forty archers from Viera. Behind them were fifty sword maidens. All were clad in leather armor and ready to do battle.

A broad smile spread across the king's face. "I am most grateful you've come," he said. "Lieutenant," he called to a tall, skinny man standing nearby. "Show these archers to the palace roof and find a company for the sword maidens to join."

"Right away, sire," the man replied.

"My lord River," the king said. "I would have you stay behind to defend my people should our attack fail. Whatever happens to me, I know you will keep my citizens safe."

"I will do everything I can to protect them, your majesty," River replied.

The ships had already reached the shore, and the troops could be seen gathering on the deck. They were forming ranks and preparing to disembark. Aelryk and his men mounted their horses and dashed to the beach. They drew their swords in preparation for the charge.

The first ship unloaded a large portion of Ulda's army onto the sand. Aelryk gave the order, and his men raced toward the invaders, their swords held high in their hands. Behind them, Morek's men began lining up their horses for the second charge. The second ship had unloaded nearly half of its men, and the rest were quickly following. Holding up his sword, he led the charge against the second wave of invaders. The rest of Aelryk's army gathered on the beach ready to fight. Isandra and her elves led the way, followed by the sword maidens from Viera.

The remaining two ships began unloading at the same time. Isandra stared intently as the monsters gathered on the beach. She had never expected so many. The thought of so many human and animal souls being combined in forced servitude was appalling. She pitied the poor creatures, but she knew they could only be released by death. With a loud cry, she sounded the third charge and headed straight for the beasts.

Mel shouted to his archers, "Spiders! Aim for their eyes!" He knew the swords of the men below were practically useless against these beasts. There were hundreds of them, but they would not last long against the skilled archers of Viera. One by one, the spiders began to fall.

Despite the efforts of Aelryk's army, the enemy continued to advance. They vastly outnumbered the Na'zorans and were showing no signs of hesitation. The Soulbinders launched fireballs into Aelryk's ranks, destroying their formations and scattering the troops. Ulda's army fought savagely and relentlessly.

Aelryk noticed a blinding flash from the corner of his eye. Descending from one of the ships was a giant, golden, man-like creature. It moved somewhat haltingly, but that did not hinder its attack. Unwavering, Aelryk signaled his troops to advance on the golden creature. It caught sight of the king and made its way to meet him. It swung its massive arms, cutting down men and horses in its path.

Aelryk swung his sword at the giant, striking it near the waste. His sword glanced off without causing any damage. The golden form swiped at the king, knocking him from his horse. Morek, seeing that his king was in danger, rushed to his side.

Morek arrived just in time to distract the golden giant while Aelryk climbed back to his feet and onto his horse. From a palace balcony, the court mages tried desperately to subdue the giant with magic. Their efforts were in vain, and the creature continued to fight. It swung its arms wildly and kicked at the groups of men as they advanced. The archers fired at it, but the arrows refused to stick in its golden hide.

Mi'tal fought his way through a crowd of wolfbeasts to make his way to the king. He swung his mighty hammer at the giant's legs, knocking it off balance. As it staggered, he swung again, this time hitting the back of its knee. It lurched forward and could not catch itself. It hit the ground, landing hard upon its knees.

Mustering all of his strength, Aelryk drew back his runed sword and charged at the giant. River's eyes flashed blue as he concentrated his energy on the king's sword. In response, the runes etched into the blade radiated with blue light. Aelryk forced the tip deep into the giant's back. It fell backwards with a horrifying cry. As soon as it hit the ground, Aelryk dismounted his horse and thrust his sword deep into the back of the creature's neck. With a long metallic sigh, the giant let out its last breath.

The battle continued to rage all around Aelryk. Turning his attention back to the ships, he could see that more of Ulda's army had begun to disembark. Arrows whizzed wildly overhead in hopes of eliminating the reinforcements. Some of them found their targets, but still the enemy advanced. Aelryk's men were outnumbered nearly two to one and would soon be overwhelmed.

Chapter 38

River looked to the ocean and saw that more troops were still departing the ships. As he looked around the battlefield, he could tell the Na'zorans were facing certain defeat. Everywhere he looked, the enemy continued to advance while the Na'zorans struggled to hold them back.

He headed out amidst the battle to speak with the king. As he walked, he was confronted by a wolfbeast who slashed wildly at him. The blows rippled through his armor as if through water. River remained completely unharmed, and the beast looked bewildered at its inability to harm the elf. Giving up, it turned its attentions back to the Na'zoran army.

Halfway to the king, a swordsman attacked River. Again, he was unharmed. Every swing of the sword splashed off of River's armor as if it had slapped the surface of a lake. The invading army's weapons were completely useless against him. He ignored the attacker and continued until he reached the king.

"King Aelryk," he called. "You must sound the retreat."

Aelryk looked at him sternly and said, "No, we must continue to fight, or all will be lost."

"Please," River said. "You must pull them back, or you will all die here." He stared at the king, his face serious.

"We will die if we must," the king replied.

"I cannot save you if you are dead," River said with an uncommon urgency to his voice.

Aelryk looked into River's eyes, and he knew what he must do. "Sound the retreat!" he cried. The call echoed throughout the ranks, and the men began to pull away from the fighting and back towards the palace. The enemy pursued, but many of them were struck down by the archers. The rest remained on the battlefield, awaiting orders from their commanders.

"Yourself as well," River said, laying a hand on the king's shoulder.

Aelryk nodded, trusting fully in the elf. He turned and joined the rest of his army in retreat.

Isandra paused in her retreat to take a look back at her father. He stood calmly near the coastline and watched as Aelryk's army departed. Once they were safely back to the palace, he walked slowly toward the ocean, his arms outstretched. Closing his eyes, he began to speak softly to the sapphire blue waters of the sea. He called upon all of the spirits who dwelt there, issuing an urgent plea.

Aelryk watched in awe as the ocean shrank away from the shore, capsizing the ships of his enemy. An enormous wall of blue water materialized before his eyes. Driven by a strong roaring wind, the massive tidal wave rushed forward. With a thunderous crash, it crushed Ulda's army beneath it. In less than a minute the entire force was gone, swallowed by the sea.

As the water began to recede, Aelryk saw River still standing at the shoreline. All of a sudden, he fell to his knees and then landed face down in the sand. Aelryk rushed forward to aid his friend, followed closely by Isandra.

"Father!" she cried as she dismounted her horse. She ran to him, rolled his body over, and placed her ear to his chest. "He's still alive," she said.

Aelryk helped Isandra lift River onto her horse. She rode quickly back to the palace to get her father inside. She did not know if he would survive, but she was determined to find all the help she could. Every healer in Na'zora would attend him, or they would answer to her. She would not let her father die.

* * * * *

River awoke on a soft feather bed in Aelryk's palace. Isandra, who had not left his side, grasped his hand as he sat up.

"Father," she said. "You're finally awake."

"How long was I asleep?" he asked.

"Two days," Aelryk replied. He had just entered the room hoping to check on his friend. "It's good to have you with us again."

"What happened out there?" Isandra asked.

"I asked the spirits in the ocean to release those whose souls had been bound by evil. We combined our strength to form the wave, and it seems the wind itself lent its mighty hand. The sea did not differentiate between those who served Ulda willingly and those who were taken by force. They are all free now."

"Why did you collapse?" she asked.

"Exhaustion," he said. "This body has its limits, and they are many. If I live another thousand years, I will never have the strength to perform such a feat again."

"I'm just glad you're alive," she replied, laying her head on her father's shoulder.

"You have saved us all," Aelryk said. "I am eternally indebted to you. Words cannot express my gratitude."

"You asked me to keep your people safe. I did the best that I could," he replied. Getting up from the bed, he added, "I must pay tribute to the sea."

Isandra walked with him back to the coast where he waded into the calm blue waters. As of yet, none of the bodies of the invading army had washed ashore, and the beach showed no signs of a recent battle. She watched as he conversed with the unseen spirits and walked back and forth along the coastline. When he rejoined her, he said, "There is now a magical barrier of protection at Na'zora's coastline. Never again will they be attacked by sea."

A glint in the sand caught Isandra's eye. She moved toward the shiny object and began kicking away the sand with her boot. The golden suit that had once housed a giant lay bent and twisted on the beach. She pulled the gold out of the sand and carried it back inside to place before the king in his council chambers.

"This gold will be used to aid those who have been most affected by this war," the king said. "It cannot replace those who were lost, but it may help provide for their families." Aelryk turned to his councilors and said, "We must also do what we can to assist the citizens of Al'marr in rebuilding their homeland. Much has been taken from them, and I would help them in any way possible. Councilor Loren, you will travel to Al'marr to assess the situation. Try to find any surviving member of their royal house, no matter how distant. They are going to need true leadership to repair their kingdom."

Chapter 39

"No!" Ulda shouted as he gazed into his orb.

"No! No! This cannot be happening!" He shook his head and slammed the orb to the floor in his anger. His entire army was obliterated. He had nothing left.

The day his army had set sail for Na'zora, the miners of Al'marr had began an uprising. They had gathered and marched on his palace demanding that he step down and leave their kingdom for good. So far, he had ignored them. Without his army, however, he would have little chance to quell the uprising. Alone he could only hope to take out a few hundred of them before he was overwhelmed.

Ulda hung his head in defeat. Sighing, he rose from his seat and began collecting the few items from his laboratory that he would be able to carry to his ship. His only choice was to flee. He could not hope to hold Al'marr with his army and allies dead. As long as the ship had not been taken by the rebels, he would be able to return to Ral'nassa.

He scooped the fallen orb from the floor and placed it gently inside his knapsack. He gathered a few more scrolls and as many gems as he could find. Taking in a deep breath and letting it out forcefully, he threw open the doors leading into the hallway. He marched towards the palace entrance, his footsteps echoing throughout the palace.

As he reached the main entrance, he turned and gave a look behind. Everywhere he looked, he saw unfulfilled ambitions. His anger began to boil over, and he turned and kicked open the door to the front courtyard. The crowd of rebels stood stunned for a moment. They had not expected him to come outside. Within seconds, they began rushing towards him. Their faces were determined, their intentions clear. Ulda would die by their hands.

He took one look at the crowd and laughed. "You are no match for me. You are no more than dirt beneath my feet." He raised a hand to touch his necklace and let forth an enormous energy burst. The wave radiated among the crowd, knocking the majority of them off their feet. Ulda hurried down the slopes toward the shore before the stunned mob could follow. He was relieved to see that his ship was still there awaiting his arrival.

As he boarded the ship, he was greeted by its captain. "Welcome aboard, your majesty," he said. "Has the battle gone well? Shall we head for Na'zora?"

"There's been a change in plans," Ulda replied. "Take me to Ral'nassa."

He went below decks to his quarters and laid his few belongings on his dresser. The ship began to pull away from the shore, and he knew that he would be safe now. The cargo area was filled with the remaining gold that had been mined, and hundreds of gems had been packed inside as well. These precious items would give him the new start he desperately needed. He had nothing in Ral'nassa but enemies. Still, it was home. In Ral'nassa, he would begin again.

Chapter 40

In honor of their victory, Aelryk ordered every citizen of Na'zora to celebrate. Every worker was to be given the day off and allowed to spend the day in the manner of their choosing. A feast was laid out at the palace, and hundreds of people were in attendance. River, Mel, and General Morek were given places of honor among the attendees. Isandra and Mi'tal were also recognized for their bravery and skill in battle.

Music filled the palace dining hall as the ceremonies began. Aelryk, dressed in his finest red tunic, proposed a toast. "To all of you who fought so bravely to destroy the evil that threatened us. To Mel for providing us with much-needed archers, and to Isandra, Councilor Mi'tal, and General Morek for their leadership and skill. May we never forget Lord

River and the spirits of the sea. They are responsible for ridding us of this evil for good. We drink to you!"

The crowd cheered and lifted their glasses high. The ale flowed freely, and the decadent foods were served. Many guests joined each other in dancing. With laughter and song, the celebration continued deep into the night. Most of the guests would spend the night in various locations around the palace. Many of them lay where their bodies had finally succumbed to exhaustion brought on by the merry-making.

The following morning, Mel requested an audience with the king. He was ready to make a few requests on behalf of his people.

"Good morning, Mel," the king began. "I trust you slept well."

"I did, your majesty," he replied.

"You have done me a great service, young elf. What would you ask of this king as payment?"

"I would ask, your highness, that the lands forcefully taken from the Silver Birch Clan be returned to them."

Aelryk leaned forward on his throne and clasped his hands together in front of him. "You do realize most of that has been converted to farmland. I doubt it would be of much use to hunters and gatherers."

"Some of my people may wish to learn about farming. If so, they should be given that opportunity. Otherwise, I will restore the forests with the help of the dryads."

"So be it," the king replied. "Mi'tal will make the arrangements for our citizens to be moved. The Silver Birch Clan will be placed under the protection of Na'zora, and you are granted all the same privileges as free citizens of my kingdom. You will continue to govern yourselves, and you will pay no taxes to the realm."

"Thank you, my lord," Mel said. "There is one more thing."

Aelryk raised an eyebrow. "Yes?"

"We object to being referred to as the Wild Elves. It implies we are uncivilized. From now on, we wish to be called the Woodland Elves."

"As you wish," the king replied.

Mel had no intention of bowing to anyone, so he nodded his head in respect instead. He rejoined his clansmen and proceeded home to the Forests of Viera. With their former lands returned to them, they no longer risked overhunting as their population grew. They would thrive within the forests of their ancestors.

River and Isandra were making preparations to leave as well. King Aelryk, Lisalla, and Rykon joined them near the royal stables to bid them farewell.

"I can never thank you enough, my friend," the king said.

They grasped each other's forearms, and River placed an oval-shaped sapphire in the king's hand. It was deep blue and suitably sized for a ring. "You may use this should you ever wish to contact me again."

Aelryk looked down at the sparkling gem in his hand. "I hope we shall meet again someday," he said.

"We shall," River replied. He paused for a moment, his eyes looking off to the side at nothing in particular. "I do not know why I will make the journey. It will be years from now, and it will be winter here."

"Winter is when they bring up all of the fine chocolates from Enald," the king said with a grin.

"Then I shall look forward to it," River said.

The elves mounted their horses and gave a last wave to say goodbye to their friends. As they headed west, the air became crisper and cooler, and the scent of spring flowers drifted on the wind. The Vale was calling to them as it patiently waited to welcome them home.

About the Author

Lana Axe lives in the Missouri countryside surrounded by dogs, cats, birds and reptiles. She spends most of her free time daydreaming about elves, magic, and far-away lands.

For more information, please visit:
http://lana-axe.com/